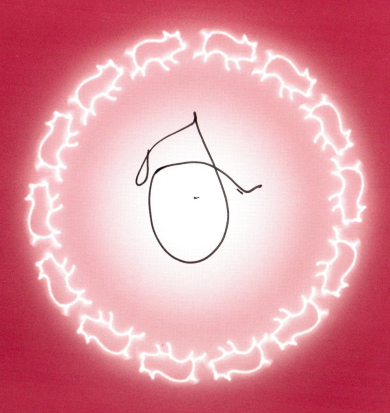

This special signed edition
is limited to 850 numbered copies
and 26 lettered copies.

This is copy

474

PIGGS

PIGGS

NEAL BARRETT, JR.

SUBTERRANEAN PRESS ◆ 2002

Piggs
Copyright © 2002 by Neal Barrett, Jr.
All rights reserved.

Dustjacket and interior illustrations
Copyright © 2002 by Don Ivan Punchatz.
All rights reserved.

Interior design
Copyright © 2002 by Tim Holt. All rights reserved.

FIRST EDITION
January 2002

ISBN
1-931081-23-9

Subterranean Press
P.O. Box 190106
Burton, MI 48519

email:
publisher@subterraneanpress.com

website:
www.subterraneanpress.com

PIGGS

ONE...

What we could do," the man said, "we've got stuff going through Bossier City up to Big D. This is maybe week, week after next, we let you know when. We offload a partial, you come and get it, we hold the rest."

"I don't want a partial," Cecil said. "I don't think I said partial anywhere."

"I don't think you did," the man said. "The partial thing, that's temporary. That's a one-time thing is what it is."

"Temporary till what?" Cecil knew what, but he went ahead and asked. You don't ask, the guy'd think you didn't know better, so Cecil had to ask.

One of the girls finished up. The crowd began to hoot and yell. The strobe lights exploded into purple, white and red.

"You know, we get paid, you get the partial," the man said. "Everything goes down, you get the rest."

"I lay out, I'm paying for the whole thing, you gimme half. This is how it looks to me."

The man leaned across the table. "You get *all* of it, Mr. Dupree. Two, three days outside. We're not looking to inconvenience you. This is just business, this is no big thing. You've been around so you ought to know that."

The guy, he'd stepped right in it, gone across the line. Cecil didn't show it, but anyone who knew about Cecil could have told the guy that.

"I'm a bidnessman myself," Cecil said. "We got a misunderstanding, I'd like to clear it up. Ambrose and me, we go back to eighty-six. He had the club in Houston, I had a place next door. We've done a lot of bidness, there's never been a problem with either him or me."

"Mr. Ambrose is retired. You know him, you know he's not well, you know he's not active in the business anymore."

"I know he's not active. I know he's got serious problems with his parts. I know he's got a dick is going to maybe fall off onna floor, so what's that got to do with me?"

"It's a one-time thing, it's just temporary."

"I got that, I got it the first couple times it come around."

Cecil looked at Grape. Grape was where he always was, at a table near the booth. Grape looked asleep. He looked like a tick dog, sleeping on a hot front porch.

"I'd like another bock," Cecil said. "I'd like to get it cold this time. Get our guest a refill, whatever he's having, get him some of that."

The man looked relieved. He didn't like how things were going, he was ready for a break. He said he'd like to go to the john if Grape would show him where.

"Show him," Cecil said, and Grape got up and led him off, through the tables past the bar.

◆ ◆ ◆

Once he was out of sight of Cecil, Kenny let out a breath. It was cold in the place, but he tended to sweat.

8

PIGGS

The motel was cheap and the water wasn't hot. Kenny couldn't take a shower, he couldn't handle that. He'd washed beneath his arms, put on a clean shirt, now the shirt was wringing wet.

Jesus, he thought, what am I doing here, what is Junior thinking about, dealing with a clown like this? The guy is a nutcase, a geek, an absolute freak.

He knew it the minute he saw Dupree, the guy over fifty, maybe fifty-five. Big country ears and bad teeth. A tall and skinny guy, no fat at all. And wearing—get this—no shirt and fucking overalls.

Kenny wasn't fooled a minute. Okay, a minute and a half. The farmer suit and the goofball smile couldn't hide the eyes. Couldn't hide the mean in those awful septic eyes. He'd seen a couple dudes like Cecil down in Baton Rouge. Guys in Boston, that didn't look like him at all. It was something you could smell, something you knew if you'd been around a while. You could hide maybe anything, but you couldn't hide the eyes.

And *this* guy, holy shit. On top of the cornball act, you can't help looking at the guy, the guy's got a problem, the guy's got a problem with his face. You don't know where to look, so you start looking everywhere else. You look back again, he sees you doing that. Maybe, if they'd ever do the deal, he could start on back. Get out of Hick City, drive for a while, find a real motel. Whatever. As long as he didn't have to see the fucking hayseed again, and he wouldn't mind telling Junior that.

❖ ❖ ❖

Cat Eye stood where he always did, just to Cecil's right.

Cecil didn't have to look, Cecil knew the Cat was there. It's morning, it's the middle of the night, the Cat's going to be there, this is what the Cat's for.

9

Out across the room, the crowd cheered again. One of the girls was coming on, the short one from Waco that everybody liked, though Cecil couldn't see why. You look at naked girls for a while, they tend to look alike. Tits and legs and ass, you got a different shape, you got a different size. You're looking all the time, they're looking all alike.

Unless, Cecil thought, you got something special, something doesn't even have a name, but you know that something's there. Gloria had it, and Cecil knew it the minute she walked in the door. He knew it, and the jerkoffs sitting in the dark, they knew it too. She was headliner stuff. She had that quality you couldn't define. The closest Cecil came was the very first night she went on.

"Son of a bitch," Cecil said to Grape, "that kid has got it, that kid is nakeder than anybody else I ever seen…"

❖ ❖ ❖

Cecil watched the man go. He was forty, maybe, stocky and under five-ten, a man who'd played ball some time, and now all the muscle was sliding into fat.

He was dressed for being anywhere else. For sure not Mexican Wells, or anyplace else in Garner County, Texas, and for certain not in Piggs. Nobody wore loafers in Piggs, for Christ's sake, loafers with a tassel on top. Loafers and dress pants, a shirt and a tie. The shirt was okay, a good shade of blue, but the collar was white. Cecil liked shirts that were all one color. You want a white shirt, go ahead and do it, do the whole thing white.

Cecil didn't like him, didn't like him from the start. Didn't like his shirt, didn't like his attitude. Down in New Orleans, he was just another heavy, but send him up here, he thought he was maybe something else. Also, the guy had looked at Cecil's face. Not right at him, but out of the corner of his eye, Cecil had caught him at it twice.

PiGGS

His name was Hutt Kenny. Not Kenny first, but the other way around. Hutt, he said, though nobody asked. Hutt stood for Hutton, but no one called him that. Cecil was certain no one in the state of Louisiana had a name like Hutton Kenny. Boston, maybe, or Rhode fucking Island, but nowhere in New Orleans. Which meant the old man was really out of the picture. That his boy was bringing new people in from out of state. People from the East. People with names where Kenny came last. That was depressing, Cecil thought, but everything changed, nothing ever stayed the same.

There was some kind of trouble, an angry swell above the usual bedlam at the bar, a brief discord that quickly faded away. Cecil paid it no mind, not until Grape came back with Kenny in tow. Kenny was mad, holding it back, but you could see it in his eyes. You been around a while, you can see it in the eyes.

"What's the problem?" Cecil said, talking to Grape, not talking to Hutt.

"Nothing," Hutt said, "no big deal."

"Ol' boy called him a fag," Grape said. "Said he was wearing funny shoes."

"Who was this now, you know who it is?"

"Skinny dude, short hair, leather jacket."

"Forget it," Hutt said, "fucker was drunk." He downed his drink, tapping the glass to get the whiskey past the ice.

"Like an aviator jacket," Cecil said, looking at the bar.

"Uh-huh, something like that."

Cecil looked at Hutt. Hutt wouldn't look back. He was clearly irritated. The girl came with drinks. She didn't have a bottom or a top. Hutt gave her a quick appraising glance, then picked up his glass and drank it down.

"Let's forget it, all right? We've got business, Mr. Dupree. That's why I drove up here, so you and me could

11

talk. I don't give a shit what the guy said, doesn't mean a thing to me."

"I give a shit," Cecil said. "This is my place, you're a guest here. That boy showed no respect to you, Mr. Kenny. Like you're showing no respect to me. I am overlooking that, I don't take offense. My guess is, you being a asshole doesn't have a thing to do with this. This is a social disorder, this is a personal failing in yourself. What I am saying, I'm saying Ambrose Junior, this is the word from him to me. Junior wants to tell me I am off his Christmas list. He'll let me do bidness, but I got to kiss his ass. I got to pretend this kid who is wet behind the ears is the fucking Godfather, thinks he's in a movie somewhere. What do you think, Mr. Kenny, am I getting close, would I be correct in saying that?"

It looked as if Hutt might strangle on his collar. His glass was empty and all he had was ice.

"This isn't right, Mr. Du-pree, now you're aware of that. This kind of talk, this won't get us anywhere at all."

"You can take that tie off you want. We like folks to feel at home here."

Cecil looked past the booth, studied the crowd at the bar, looked at the bar a long time, looked back at Hutt. Long enough for Hutt to look off at something else.

"Grape, get us some food in here," Cecil said. He stood, then, and set down his beer. "Get me a Shiner, get our guest another drink."

"Nothing for me," Hutt said.

"Get him a drink," Cecil said. "Easy on the ice. The man's from fucking Maine somewhere, he don't want a lot of ice..."

TWO...

The bar was against the west wall, the tables shoved together past that. There were two small platforms next to center stage. When a girl got through, she could climb on a platform and do her thing there. There were always three girls going all the time.

The place was packed solid, good for Tuesday night, though most nights at Piggs were like Saturdays anywhere else. Texas law said a club could serve drinks if the girls only took off a top. Bring Your Own Bottle, if the bottom came off as well.

The law applied to Garner County, the exception being Cecil Dupree, who gave of himself through personal endowments, outright bribes, and football scholarships.

The crowd was mostly male, a mixed bag of college kids, used car salesmen and men in gimme caps. Sometimes, a man would bring a woman in Piggs, hoping the kinky convolutions on stage were contagious, that a wife or a girlfriend would maybe learn something, and take it back home when she left.

Cecil wouldn't keep a woman out, but he thought it was wrong to bring them in. It made guys nervous to see a woman sitting there with all her clothes on. A guy comes to Piggs, he doesn't want to see that.

He made his way through the darkened room, keeping to the edge, avoiding the crowd as best he could. Piggs had been a seafood place before Cecil bought it out. Built-in tanks ran around three walls. The tanks had held tropical fish, but now they held pigs. This is how Piggs got its name. The pigs were cute and pink, the size of puppy dogs. People liked to watch pigs, liked to watch them romp about. A man gets tired of just watching private parts, he'll stop and watch a pig.

You could write your name on a pig for twenty bucks. This was Cecil's idea, and it brought in some nice extra cash. Your name might be next to Dolly or Garth, or maybe even Willie himself. No one stopped to think pigs grew fast. There were always pigs in the tanks, signed by ordinary people and famous country stars. Always cute, and always the very same size...

◆ ◆ ◆

It was mid-July, and the AC was high as it would go. Cecil slipped out the side door, into the hot oppressive night. He stopped and looked up at the dark and starless sky, breathed in the heated summer air. The smells were smells he liked. Tar grown soft from the fury of the day, the fumes of passing cars. He could smell the grease from Wan's, smell the tang of sour beer. There were plenty of smells in the world, but these were the ones he liked the best.

The neon sign atop the building read **PIGGS,** a sign you could read nearly three miles away. The pink letters flashed every second and a half. Circling the sign was a

14

herd of blue pigs. They chased one another in a fast and jerky pace just below the speed of light. Flashing letters and the orbital pigs played tricks upon the eye. People felt dizzy as soon as they arrived. People who were drunk had a tendency to throw up on the ground. People prone to fits didn't go to Piggs at all.

Cecil crossed the dim parking lot. He'd spotted the aviator jacket, seen the man leave, watched him go while he talked to Hutt Kenny or maybe Kenny Hutt. Talked to the asshole Ambrose Junior had sent up from New Orleans. Sent him up to insult Cecil R. Dupree, who'd been his father's friend. If the old man knew, he'd be angry and ashamed. Ambrose Senior was a standup guy. He would never allow an insult to his friends. Or maybe, Cecil thought, Ambrose wouldn't care. A man having trouble with his parts doesn't really give a shit about anybody else.

◆ ◆ ◆

Cat Eye was standing by Cecil's Cadillac, a man a little smaller than a truck, a man with little alligator eyes. Cecil hadn't asked him to follow, but that was Cat's job, to be anywhere Cecil wanted him to be.

Cecil walked to his car, which was parked in its spot against the wall. The car was extra-long and lizard-green, a super-extended '93 Caddie, big enough to haul a pro basketball team. He opened the trunk, found a burlap sack, and closed the trunk again. Cat Eye leaned against the car. A Dodge Ram roared out of the lot, spraying gravel in its wake. College boys who'd downed a few beers, seen some naked girls.

No one else was leaving, no one else was in the lot.

The man in the aviator jacket was standing by a low-slung car, looking for his keys. The car was an '84 Spyder, maybe '85. The paint was beetle-black, so deep and shiny black, the neon from Piggs was a dazzling sight to see.

The man heard Cecil walk up behind him, jerked around fast, wondered what this was all about, decided he was bigger, shook his head, said, "What the fuck, man?"

Cecil pulled a short-handled axe from his burlap sack and whipped it across the man's gut. The man cried out and staggered back, slammed against the car. He threw one hand before his face. Cecil hacked at him again. The blade took off three fingers, buried itself between the neck and the shoulders clear to the center of the chest. The man slid down, leaving dark streaks on the beetle-black car. Sat with his hands hung loose by his sides.

Cecil put his foot on the man and pulled the blade out. Dropped the axe in the sack and walked across the lot. Stopped to talk to Cat Eye, gave Cat the sack, and went back into Piggs. The AC labored on the roof, chugging away in a hopeless effort to chill the Texas night. A truck whined by, heading for 35, heading for San Antone. The headlights swept across the lot, flashed, for an instant, on a man with alligator eyes. A man with a sack by a lizard-green car.

THREE...

Hutt was looking better, more relaxed now, slumped in the booth, a couple more drinks inside him and a skinny naked girl on his lap. The color in his cheeks was partly from the drinks, partly from the fact that the girl was doing something out of sight. The girl billed herself as Alabama Straight, though Cecil doubted that. The homo persuasion was rampant in the stripping game, a fact club owners didn't care to advertise.

"I asked you to get us some food over here," Cecil said, "I don't see food anywhere."

"It's coming," Grape said, "I got you garlic shrimp."

"I don't like the garlic shrimp."

"Yeah, you do. You get it all the time."

"I used to get it, I don't get it anymore."

"I'll get you something else," Grape said.

Cecil looked at Hutt. Hutt hadn't noticed he was back. He had the girl down in the booth. The girl didn't like it, but Hutt didn't care.

"I forgot about the shrimp," Grape said. "I remember you saying, we was over to Wan's, you don't like it, the shrimp."

"Forget it. Forget about the shrimp."

"What you want me to do? He's going to nail her right there."

"What I'm going to do is nail *him*. I'm not taking a partial, that asshole don't know it yet. Leave him alone, give Alabama a twenty from me."

"There he is, there's the guy again," Grape said.

"There's who?"

"The clown, the dude called your guy a fag."

Cecil looked where Grape was pointing. "That guy's got a brown jacket. You said a black."

"No, sir. I believe I said brown. Short hair, brown jacket like the aviators wear."

"I think you said black."

"I think I said brown," Grape said.

"I'm pretty sure you said black."

"It's fuckin' dark in here, I coulda said black."

"I think that's what you did."

"Whatever," Grape said.

"The food gets here, I'll get you somethin' else. The Moo Goo and hot and sour soup."

"Moo Goo's fine," Cecil said. "Gimme a eggroll, forget the fucking soup."

FOUR...

The way the deal worked, Ortega was the waiter at Wan's, and a cook sometimes if Ahmed got high and couldn't find his head. Ortega waited tables, and hauled dishes back from out front or across the way at Piggs. The dishes and the pots wound up in Jack's sink.

The washing wasn't bad, Jack didn't mind that. The other part was what he didn't like. Cecil didn't care if the dishes got clean. Food Reclamation, that was Cecil's thing. A guy leaves half an eggroll, toss out the fried part, save the inside. Save all the rice except the part soaks up a little sauce. Save all the meat because meat costs a lot—even though Cecil buys cuts Tex Savallo couldn't give away to anybody else.

Rhino ran Wan Lee's for Cecil, and Rhino kept his eye on Ahmed, Ortega and Jack. If he didn't, Ortega and Ahmed would steal the place blind. Jack wouldn't steal, but Jack dumped scraps down the sink. Cecil wouldn't stand for that. Rhino thought Cecil was nuts. He was also plain terrified, and he did what Cecil said.

Jack couldn't stand the floaters. Floaters made him sick. A little Hunan bobs up, Jack's sure he's got to barf. It wasn't like that, before he went down for five to ten. He only did three, but that was enough to do him in. Huntsville soured him inside and out. Now he had irritated bowel syndrome and gastro- this and that. He used to eat chili and barbecue and pizza twice a week. Now white rice was a culinary treat. Jack looked in the mirror sometimes, certain his eyes were slanting up at both ends. He dreamed about salsa and Habeñero peppers, and woke up sweating with a fire in his belly that he couldn't put out. Sometimes, early in the morning, the dreams got better than that. Sometimes he was back in Oke City, driving down Western in a Park Avenue, some babe on the leather there beside him, a babe with legs up to here. Her name escaped him now, he'd never been any good at that.

Rhino came through the swinging doors and said, "Couple garlic shrimp, lemon chicken, egg rolls, hot and sour soup. No scraps or nothing, this is for Cecil, this ain't for out front."

"Is okay I spit in somet'in," Ahmed said, "you got a problem wi' dat?"

"No it ain't okay, raghead, it's okay with me you fuckin' die, that's what's okay with me. Jack, you take it over. Don't goof around, get it there hot."

Jack blinked. "I got dishes. I got stuff to do here."

"Uh-huh. Now you got stuff to do *there*."

"I don't want to, man."

"You don't wanta, you don't wanta what?"

"I don't want to. Let Ortega go."

Rhino closed one eye. The eye disappeared in fat.

"Ortega's the waiter, Ahmed's the cook, I'm the fuckin' maitre d'. You're what I tell you to be, you got any problem with that?"

"Hey, I don't want to, man."

Ahmed snickered. A snicker, not a laugh. A snicker and a leer he'd brought over from Iraq. Rhino gave him a look. Turned back to Jack. "Take the stuff over. Don't mess around, get your ass back." Rhino disappeared. Ahmed tossed a handful of shrimp in the wok. The wok hissed and sizzled in a cloud of peanut oil. Ahmed wore a turban that used to be white. Sweat squeezed under and wandered down his brow. Hid in his beard, then dropped in the wok.

"Hey, Cecil like you a lot," Ahmed said, "you a pretty locky guy, you know dat? What I t'ink, Jhack, I t'ink Cecil he got hees eye on you. I t'ink you in line for a very big jhob roun' here..."

Ahmed couldn't finish. His shoulders shook, and his cheeks exploded like a runaway balloon.

Jack wanted to jump the little shit, break a rib or two. Ahmed was five-two, eighty-eight wet. What he'd like to do, he'd like to ram Ahmed's head down in the wok. Hold him there till it got a good crust, till you couldn't tell Ahmed from the shrimp. He used to hand out a lot of hurt, liked to knock a guy around. But he wasn't two-ten anymore, he was one-fifty-five. His gut was screwed up and it hurt too much to hurt anybody else.

"He sees me, he'll clobber me or something," Jack said. "He don't like me going over there, he likes me stayin' here. Fuck, Rhino knows that. He's going to get me killed, that's what he's gonna to do."

"I t'ink you very wrong about Cecil," Ahmed said. "Cecil like you, Jhack." He blew a wet kiss in the air. "He maybe goin' to give you a ring, sometin' like dat."

"All you got, you got this one fucking act," Jack said. "Why don't you take a day off, try and work up something else?"

Ahmed rolled his eyes, like he'd seen Arabs do on TV. Whipped a herd of shrimp around the wok, gave them a squirt of chili oil. Slid them on a plate. Started all over. Cooked a batch of chicken. Gave everyone a scoop of pasty rice, egg rolls he'd never used at all.

"Here you go, man. Lemon chick'n, garlic shrim'. What you t'ink Cecil having, hah? I am guessin' shrim'. Gotta be de shrimp, man. I can't spit on everyti'ng at once."

◆   ◆   ◆

The throughway from Wan's to the back door of Piggs was an open alleyway. Wan's walls were brick, painted whorehouse red. Piggs' walls were corrugated tin. In between the two was a Dumpster full of smells. Smells from the Orient, smells from the West. Chinese cabbage, onions and shrimp. Beer, whiskey, and petrified chips. Jack could hardly stand the smells fresh, he couldn't tolerate them dead.

The stench was stupefying in the dreadful heat of day. The smells didn't go away at night. At 11:22, the temperature in Mexican Wells was just under ninety-eight.

Jack knew how to hold his breath, Jack could hold his breath for some time. He had held it for three whole years in the Huntsville pen. Held it in the cells, in the crowded corridors, held it in the john. Never took a breath in the big mess hall. A little sniff there would make him sicker than a dog.

He thought about Ahmed. He wished he had the nerve to do something bad to Cecil's plate. Jack hated Ahmed, but Ahmed had guts, you had to give him that. Ahmed had grown up in the desert. He'd shown Jack where on a map. All he had to eat was ants, Ahmed said, he didn't have any shoes or socks. No wonder he wasn't scared of anything at all.

Jack stopped, halfway through the alleyway. He heard this sound, like a pipe had maybe broken, like someone had left a faucet on. He looked to his right and saw it wasn't that at all. Some asshole was standing in the dark, pissing on the wall.

"Hey, cut that out," Jack said, "goddamnit, we got rest rooms for that."

The guy kept pissing, he didn't look at Jack. Jesus, Jack thought, he must've been in Piggs all night.

"I'm not telling you again, just stop it right now. I can send people out here, you know."

"Fhugga you..." the guy said in the dark.

"Okay, that's it. You've had it, pal—"

With that, Jack forgot what he was doing, forgot he was talking, and took a deep breath. Kung Po chicken, Szechuan pork, margaritas past their prime. Jack bolted for the door, shut it behind him, sucked in a breath, grateful for the stale and smoky air of Piggs.

Light assailed his senses, music blasted from the worn-out speakers on the wall. On the main center stage, a very tall and naked girl writhed in an agony of need, squirmed in a fever of unrequited lust. The message, from the fire in her eyes, from her damp and parted lips, said all she really wanted was a night of sweaty love. Love with a loser, love with a bald guy dreaming of her crotch. Plumbers in workpants, lawyers in suits, adenoidal boys. Guys who drove Jaguars, guys who drove Fords.

Jack, though, knew they didn't have a chance. The girl in the hot pink light was Gloria Mundi, the loveliest woman Jack had ever seen, ever imagined in his dreams. A woman, Jack knew, from personal encounters with Gloria herself, who possessed an inner beauty that even surpassed the outer part.

Jack was next to certain they would marry in the spring. Or possibly the summer, or maybe in the fall. Or, if not, possibly after that.

FIVE...

"Take it back," Cecil said, "get it out of here."

"Do what?" Jack said.

"Take it back, I don't want the fucking shrimp."

"You don't want it."

"You heard him," Grape said, "He says he don't want it, you listening or what?"

"Okay," Jack said.

"Okay, what?"

"Okay, I'll take it back."

"That's terrific," Grape said, "I'm glad to hear it, Jack. Mr. Dupree'll be glad you can handle this for him, he appreciates that."

Cecil had forgotten he was there. He was off somewhere, his mind on something else. Jack picked up his plate. Left the other shrimp for Grape. Set the lemon chicken in front of a man he'd never seen before. When he set the plate down, he spotted Alabama Straight. Alabama was busy down in the guy's lap.

"This any good?" the guy said.

"Yes sir, it is," Jack said.

The man speared a piece of chicken and sniffed. Jack saw he wore a tie. His shirt was blue but his collar was white. He wondered if the collar came off. They did that in Westerns sometimes, he didn't know they did it now.

Jack felt a little itch, turned and looked behind his back. Grape was where he always was, but the Cat wasn't there. He didn't miss Cat Eye, Cat wasn't anyone you'd miss. Still, if you knew where he was, you wouldn't be thinking he'd jump out at you, scare you half to death.

The girl came up for air. The guy in the tie ate his hot and sour soup. Jack got Cecil's tray and took off.

Cecil said, "Jacko, where you going with that?"

Jack stopped. Cecil was looking in his beer, he didn't look at Jack.

"Taking stuff back," Jack said. "You said take it back."

"I didn't tell you take it back."

Jack took a deep breath. "See I thought you did. I thought you didn't want the shrimp."

"You are mistaken, Jacko, I didn't say that."

"Mr. Dupree, he just told you," Grape said. "Why you want to aggravate the man?"

"No, sir. I wouldn't do that."

"Then put it *down,*" Cecil said, "you think you can manage that?"

"I'll leave it right here," Jack said, "I'll just put 'er right down."

He set the plate down, backed off fast, felt his gut tighten up again. Wondered why he was too slow to get it, too slow to see it coming every time.

"I think you might have a hearing loss," Cecil said. "You might want to see about that."

"I think that's what he's got," Grape said.

"It seems to me he does."

26

PIGGS

"You go up to Austin," Grape said, "they got a good man up there. Minnie got a thing put in, you can't even see it in her ear."

"You go and do it," Cecil said. "Get something in your ear."

"Yes, sir," Jack said. He wondered where this was going, if he'd maybe have to stand there all night. It could happen easy, Cecil had made him do awful stuff before. Cecil and Grape one night, drunk and betting twenty dollar bills, betting on how much water Jack could drink before he had to pee. Cat Eye standing there, interested or not, you never knew for sure, maybe still back in 1986, stuck in Round Two.

And Jack, recalling this event, was too slow again. Cecil looked up from his beer, turned around and caught Jack looking right at him, looking at his face.

"What you think, Jacko, I look okay to you?"

The pain in his belly nearly took him down.

"Yes sir, Mr. Dupree, you look fine to me."

"I'm pleased I do, Jack."

"Yes, sir," Jack said, and wished he hadn't said it twice.

"Well good. We got it all settled now?"

"Yes sir, Mr. Dupree."

"Then get this goddamn Chink food out of here and get the fuck out of here yourself. I would like you out of my fucking sight."

Jack didn't answer, Jack knew better than that. He picked up the shrimp, looked across the table at the guy in the blue and white shirt. The guy was trying hard to be anywhere else. It was clear that he didn't care for Piggs. He liked what the girl was doing fine, but he didn't have to drive up to Texas for that, they could do that in New Orleans.

❖ ❖ ❖

27

Jack went straight to the john and flushed the garlic shrimp. Stuck his head in the sink and turned the water on. Blotted his face with paper towels, ran his fingers through his hair. The guy in the mirror looked back. Whoever it was, it wasn't him. No big surprise. The dope in the mirror hadn't been him for some time.

Jack McCooly had never had Hollywood looks, but he wasn't the ugliest boy in town. He knew, though, he was maybe the toughest, which worked out fine in Shawnee, Oklahoma, for a flat-nose Choctaw-Irish kid. He'd had the weight then, and the muscle tone as well. Jack could take care of himself, handle any trouble, anyone that came along.

Huntsville prison had taken care of that. The ache in his gut had taken off the weight. Black dudes and skinheads had taken off the tough, shown him what tough was all about.

Nothing had ever shaken Jack like that. Not even his daddy leaving when he was ten. Before they locked him up, Jack would have crippled an asshole like Grape. Back then he would've plowed into Cat. Cat would have killed him, but Jack would have never backed down. Now, all he had was a hollow inside, a gut full of anger and rice. They'd taken something from him that was hard to get back.

He'd do it, though, he was certain of that. Work out, get himself in shape. Get a haircut, a nice pair of pants. Get a good sport shirt, a yellow or a red.

In his head he had a four-fold goal: Get his gut in shape, get his body back. Get some real money somehow. Kill Cecil and Grape, possibly the Cat. And Four, pull it off so you didn't get caught. That was a must, because he sure as shit wasn't going back inside again.

He had to pull it off. Gloria was special, she wasn't some bimbo off the street. You had to prove yourself to a woman like that. A woman like that, she wouldn't give her body and her heart to any wimp. You want the very best, you got to be the best yourself...

SIX...

Minnie Mouth was coming off, Wilda Hare was going on. Minnie would move to pole two. Laura Licks would go to three.

Which meant that Gloria was in the dressing room. Which wasn't a dressing room at all, just four by eights slapped together off the ladies' restroom.

Jack knocked, didn't wait for an answer, opened the door and went in.

"Jesus, Jack, we are naked in here!" Maggie Thatch glared, plucked a Kleenex and covered up her parts.

"You maybe didn't notice," Jack said, "but you're naked out there."

"That is professional naked, that is the entertainment portion of my life. It is personal time back here."

"I'm not looking."

"Hell you're not, you're looking right now."

"You smell like garlic," Gloria said. "I wish you wouldn't bring it in here."

"I had to see you. Before you got off."

"I don't ever get off. What for?"

31

Jack looked at Maggie. "Forget it," Maggie said, "I'm not going anywhere, just pretend I'm not here."

Maggie Thatch wasn't Jack's ideal. Jack didn't like girls with shitty attitudes. She billed herself as a Brit, but got off the bus from Fort Worth. Short, sassy, redhead all over and wiry as a squirrel, she took it all off except a tiny Union Jack, which somehow emerged at the end of her act and began to wave about, Maggie, meanwhile, standing on her head, the music shifting from Tom T. Hall to *God Save the Queen*. She did this six times a night, and it never failed to bring the house down.

"Jack, you don't look good," Gloria said, leaning in close to the mirror, sketching a tiny red line at the corner of her mouth. "You feeling all right?"

"Cecil, you know how he gets, he's got a business guy. He's got a guy in, he's got a deal going it gets him upset."

"Cecil isn't *upset,*" Maggie said. "Cecil is crazy as shit, babe."

"He said, Jacko, take the food back, then he said don't, leave the food here. You said take it back, I said. He said, I never said that. I'll tell you what, I'm tired of putting up with this crap. I had a mind to toss that shrimp right in his face."

"Ho-ho, you wish," Maggie said.

Gloria gave her a look, painted another little line at the other corner of her mouth. She was wearing a robe, a sheer black number you could nearly see through. Most of the girls brought ratty robes from home, robes that looked like old bedspreads, but Gloria had more class than that.

That was how she danced, too, in the classic style, no dumb gimmicks like Maggie and her flag, or Whoopie LaCrane, who hopped around the stage till her feathers came out. That wasn't Gloria's style. Gloria got up there and *danced.* Danced like a whisper, flinging her long hair about, letting it wash across her body like a spiderweb veil, closing her eyes like she wasn't even there, like the dance was all a dream.

Every man wanted her, wanted to take her to a bad motel, take her to a trailer, take her anywhere. Every man who saw her had the same hunger, the very same need. But nobody loved her, wanted her forever, nobody cared like Jack McCooly did.

"Cecil's got Alabama out there," Jack said. He'd thought about not saying anything at all, but Alabama was Gloria's friend. "I don't know if you saw her, but I thought you ought to know."

"I saw her," Gloria said, looking past the mirror, looking through her image there at nothing at all.

"She don't have to do it," Maggie said. "You don't ever have to do it, you can always tell 'em no."

Gloria gave her a killing look. "You don't have to *work,* either, you don't want to eat a whole lot."

"I would walk out of here before I'd do that."

"Girl, Alabama has been about everywhere else, she hasn't got anywhere to go."

"I'm just saying," Maggie said.

"Well don't."

"Excuse fucking me, okay?"

"You're fucking excused. Now shut the fuck up."

Maggie made little words with her mouth but she didn't let them go. Turned away, slipped into a G-string and a bra. The music shook the walls. Helen Reddy did *I Am Woman,* which was Laura Licks' song.

"I was thinking," Jack said, "maybe, you feel like it when you get off, we could get a coffee somewhere. I mean if you feel okay."

Gloria ran a brush through her hair. "God, Jack, that's going to be about two."

"I know it is. Everything'll be closed in town, we could go up to Denny's on I-35."

"Denny's."

"You don't like Denny's, we could go anywhere else."

"I don't mind Denny's, they got a good pie."

"You like the ice box or the hot?"

"I kinda like the hot."

"Me too. So you think it'd be all right, we could maybe do that?"

"I am real tired, Jack." She reached back and squeezed his hand. "Some other time, okay?"

Jack felt it going, felt it slip away. "I'm off on Thursdays, how about then?"

"I can't, hon. Thursday's not good for me. We'll do it some time, hear?"

Jack thought about Sunday, didn't want to hear no again. Helen Reddy quit. Tom T. Hall came on with *Jesus and Me.* Maggie got up, grabbed a sequin gown, wriggled into red spike heels.

"I hate to leave we're talking pie," Maggie said, "someone's got to work around here."

"Do it to 'em," Gloria said.

Maggie winked at Jack, slipped out the door.

"I better go too," Jack said. "Rhino'll be pissed, I don't get back."

"I'm awful sorry, Jack. Both of us working, it's real hard to work something out."

"Yeah, I guess. If we were doing something else, it wouldn't have to be like this."

"Like what?"

"You know. Some kinda work wasn't here. I expect you think I been washing dishes all my life. I can do something else. And you wouldn't have to do this."

Gloria put down her brush, turned and looked him in the eye. "I *like* doing this. I am a professional dancer, you ever notice that? Why would I want to be doing something else? You are talking awful funny, Jack."

Jack saw it in her eyes, saw he'd backed himself in a corner somehow. Wondered just how he'd done that, just how he'd get out.

"It wasn't anything, I was thinking is all."

"Well don't, okay? I don't like you doing that. You get to thinking, you act real creepy sometimes. Just be yourself, Jack."

Gloria stood, her back still to Jack. Didn't say a thing, just let the robe slip from her shoulders, fall down her back, down past her hips, past her ankles with a sigh.

Jack felt his heart stop. He could see her, he could smell her, he could reach out and touch her if he dared. He was inches from a woman without a single blemish, a woman airbrushed at birth, a woman who was perfect everywhere. He'd seen her like this a hundred times before, and so had everybody else. Still, every time it happened, it seemed like a personal private thing, something she did just for him.

Gloria turned to the left and then the right, watching herself in the mirror, watching herself with a critical eye. She brushed dark hair across her shoulders, down across her breasts, wet her lips and blinked her eyes.

"You look real good," Jack said.

"Shoot, tell me something I don't know, hon."

◆ ◆ ◆

Jack nearly bumped into Ricky Chavez. Chavez was standing by the door. Bay Rum and Listerine. Salt and pepper hair. Heavy but solid, two-twenty-two. Fringed leather jacket, big gold buckle on a tooled leather belt. Python boots with gold across the toes. A dozen red roses in his left hand, chocolates in his right.

"What do you want," Jack said, plainly irritated, knowing exactly what this jerk was up to. "You're not supposed to be back here. This area's restricted to authorized personnel."

Chavez smiled. "I am calling on the Señorita Mundi. What are you doing here, Jack?"

"I'm an employee, I'm supposed to be here."

"In the dressing room."

"In the dressing room or anywhere else my duties take me to. Patrons got to sit out front, I don't have to explain this shit to you."

"I am not a patron tonight. Tonight I am come in the role of the *galan*."

"You do what?"

"I am here as a suitor, an admirer of the lovely Gloria Mundi. I come to pay her court."

"Jesus Christ," Jack said, "get your ass out of here."

"I would speak to the lady myself."

"Huh-unh, that woman's undressed," Jack said, blocking Chavez' path, "just get on back where you belong."

"Yes, I see."

Chavez set his bouquet and chocolates on the floor. Grabbed up Jack by the elbows, and set him down again, this time away from the door.

"*Perdón,* no offense," Chavez said. "I do not wish to cause distress."

"Well goddamnit, you are," Jack said. His stomach went bad. He wanted to kill this fancy-dress greaser, but he knew he wasn't ready, not yet.

"I can throw you out of here, pal. I don't want to have to do that."

"And I do not wish you to, Jack." He gazed at Jack with his black agate eyes. The eyes said Chavez was a patient man, but a man who did what he wanted to, nearly all the time.

"I'm letting you go this time," Jack said. "Don't think you're getting away with something, 'cause you're not."

"I am grateful for your kindness, *Señor.*"

"Yeah, well those roses don't come from a real flower shop. You can get 'em down at Come-'n-Go. That woman knows flowers, she's going to know that."

Jack stomped off in the dark, stopped, and faced Chavez again.

"And you can get that candy at the fucking drug store, you can get it on sale."

With that, he was gone, out of the shadows into the hemorrhage of flashing red and white, into the whoops and the hoots and the yells, into the world of illusion and desire, into the circle of pink and smoky light where Maggie, in a moment, would reveal just how, and show exactly where, the flag of the Empire hardly ever sets...

SEVEN...

Cat Eye was confused.

This was the normal state of life in Cat's world, one he didn't think about a lot. Most of the time, he didn't have to think at all. Mr. Cecil took care of that. Mr. Cecil knew what Cat needed. Cat needed food, but he didn't care what. He needed to sleep. Mr. Cecil gave him a cot. He liked TV, but Mr. Cecil said it would rot out his eyes, and Cat didn't want to do that. Once, he'd liked to do a woman sometimes. Now, when the urge reached his head, he took care of that with one of Grape's magazines.

The problem that night, in the parking lot at Piggs, was Cat had to think for himself. What happened, was, Mr. Cecil told him what to do with the guy, the guy that he'd offed with an axe. Cat Eye understood that. Stuff like that, this is what he did best.

He was dragging the guy by his heels, taking him where he had to go, everything was fine. That's when he looked up, saw the dude pissing on the wall, saw him zipping up his pants. Saw the guy turn and see *him*.

The man was a drunk, he could hardly stand up. Still, Cat Eye knew that a man could be drunk and remember what he'd seen. And what he'd seen was Cat, Cat and a stiff that was very clearly dead, a stiff that left two dark stripes as he trailed across the lot. Which meant Cat would have to get a hose and clean the mess himself. Now there was the other guy, too, and he'd have to handle that.

The best thing to do, Cat thought, and the answer came quicker than an answer had any right to do, the best thing to do was make sure you did it right: Make sure the pisser didn't leak any too. Then you don't have another mess, you don't have to hose twice.

Cat felt good that he'd thought up the answer by himself. Thinking wasn't bad at all. It was really kind of fun, but you wouldn't want to do it all the time.

EIGHT...

Maggie Thatch was coming off. Bankers, spankers, termite inspectors, cowboys and truckers stood and cheered. They pelted the stage with dollar bills. Naked girls pranced among the sinners with overpriced beer. Guys who'd been laid off just the week before, tipped like princes for a feel.

Jack knew the routine well. Lights go down. Heavy metal up. A beat that shakes your gut. DJ swallows the mike and says "Here comes what's-her-name, right from the pages of *Playboy* magazine." Either that, or a carhop straight from Abilene.

He knew that he'd stayed too long, that Rhino would have his ass for that. He could try to make it back through the tables, out to the alley, back to the kitchen at Wan's. Only now it was break time, letting the girls sell a drink, letting the guys buy a lap dance before the next set.

If he tried to go now, Cecil might spot him, haul him back in, make him do something godawful, anything that popped in his head. Jack didn't care to risk that.

Sticking to the shadows near the side of the stage, he made his way up to the bar, past the only wall that wasn't full of baby pigs. The bartender's name was Phylla. Phylla was fully dressed, which was fine with the help, and the customers too. Phylla had gotten out of stripping in 1953.

Jack crawled past her, past the worn slats that smelled of rotgut and beer. Past rusty bobby pins, onions, olives, and ancient lemon peels.

"Phylla," Jack said, "don't say a thing, don't even look down here."

"Hi, Jack," Phylla said, "what you doin', hon?"

"Thanks, Phylla. I'm fine, how are you?"

He speeded up his crawl, picked up a splinter in his knee. Came to the end, saw the alley door. Came up slow, did a little Groucho, stayed real close to the wall. Came to the door. Reached for the knob. Cat Eye opened it, stood there staring at the floor.

Newark, Round Seven. 1988. Cat blinked, got another picture in his head. Cat said, "Hey, Jack, whachoo doin' down there?"

"Fine, how are y—"

A hand came down and lifted Jack up, held him kicking in the air. Jack didn't think, he was too scared for that. He lashed out at Cat Eye, kicked him in the crotch. Cat Eye dropped him, howled and went down. Jack scrambled up and ran. Tripped on a chair, picked it up and threw it back at Cat. The chair hit Cat and Cat didn't care.

Two doors ahead, the men's room first, storage past that. For an instant, Cat was out of sight. Jack tried the men's room. Locked. Some asshole in there doing coke, smoking pot. Jack didn't hesitate. He opened the door to the storage room and ducked inside.

Pitch black. He switched on the light, turned it off again. They used to keep beer and whiskey in there, they didn't anymore. Now they tossed in all kinds of shit, hoping someone would clean it out.

Jack stumbled over buckets and mops, old beer signs and broken panes of glass. In the back, tables without any legs were stacked on edge, enough old tables to start a new bar. Jack went to his knees again, squeezed in behind them until he found the wall.

Big, big mistake back there. Cat would have beat him up anyway, even if he hadn't fought back. But Jack had kicked him hard, and Cat Eye would kill him for that.

From the hall came a terrible sound. Anger, fury, primal rage. Cat unhappy as he beat on the walls, tore off the men's room door. Someone screamed, a scream not far from homicide.

Jack didn't move. Other sounds reached him through the door. Sounds like plumbing, sounds like pipes. Sounds like urinals ripped off the wall, toilets jerked off the floor.

Then, a sound worse than that. Nothing. No sound at all.

One...two...three... Jack counted to himself.

Cat Eye got it figured out. The door flew open. Cat stepped inside. Jack held his breath. Cat felt around and found the light. Crunched a lot of broken glass. Broke a mop across his knee. Picked up a bucket and tossed it at the wall.

"Li'l sumbitch," Cat muttered to himself, "kill the li'l shit."

Cat started on the tables. Picked them up two at a time, started tossing them aside. Jack's heart nearly stopped. Nine, ten tables deep. Three times seven, carry your eight. Cat Eye would kill him in forty seconds flat.

"Cat, what the hell you think you doing, get out of there!"

"Grape, that li'l shit, he back there somewhere, he couldn't be nowhere else."

"There isn't nobody in there but you," Grape said. "You sorry bastard, you tore up a whole bathroom, Mr. Dupree's going to have a fit."

"He's in there, Grape—"

"Get *out* of there."

"Damn, Grape—"

"Get out of there, Cat, and clean this fucking mess up!"

The lights went out. The door slammed shut. Jack didn't move. Jack was sure it was a trick.

A minute passed or an hour and a half. The music started up again, Gloria's closing number, the theme from *Burden of Proof.* It had to be one, Jack guessed, maybe even two. They'd shut the place up, bring in the cleaning crew. He wouldn't have a chance to get out until four. Then what? Cecil would wait for him to show. He wouldn't let Cat kill him, he'd think of something awful, something worse than that.

Jack tried to turn around. Going in was tight enough. There was no room at all to back out. When he tried, a nail snagged him in the butt. He wriggled away as best he could, snaked a hand behind his back. Found the nail, and something else besides. A plywood square set in the wall. Eighteen, twenty inches wide. It gave a little when he pushed.

Jack listened. Nothing but music and cheers, nothing any closer than that.

Holding his breath, he pushed the square again. Pushed a little harder, then hit it with his fist. It moved but didn't give. He raised one foot and kicked back. The panel splintered and disappeared. He could feel cool air, the smell of wet earth.

Jack pulled his foot back. The hole didn't make a lot of sense. He should be up against the outside wall, but the air was too cool for that. He reached in the hole, touched a cement wall. Reaching straight down, there was nothing at all.

A hole, then, between two walls, leading underground. It might have been a vent at one time, a shaft of some kind. Whatever it was, it was there. It didn't go to Cecil, Grape or the Cat.

Squeezing in the hole, hanging in the dark, took all the nerve he had. He'd used it all up, there wasn't any left. Jack closed his eyes. Let go and dropped in thin air...

9 NINE...

It was only two feet to the ground. He stopped and took a breath. To the right was pitch black. Where he was standing, though, was directly beneath the floor of Piggs. The floor had been there a while—little spears of light found their way through the cracks, lights of every color, dancing in a million motes of dust. Sound was hardly muffled at all. He could hear every note, from the tenor to the bass. He could hear guys yelling and stomping on the floor.

If you thought about it, the place was kinda nice. For the first time since he'd come to Mexican Wells, nobody knew where he was, no one could find him down there.

That was the thing, working for Cecil R. Dupree. Even if you had time off, Cecil was always on your ass. You couldn't get private anywhere. If he wanted you, he'd have Grape or Cat track you down. Morning, noon, middle of the night, Cecil didn't care.

It always seemed to work that way. No matter what, Jack thought, even if it started off good, it always turned out the same. Get a job, get a room, try and settle down. It lasted for a while, then the shit hit the fan and he'd take off again. Fort Worth and Lubbock, then up to Tulsa, clerking in a halfass store. He'd borrowed a twenty from the register, not any fifty, like the asshole said, meaning to pay it back. So he'd taken maybe two hundred more, and hauled out of town. All you had to do was look at this dude, he wasn't even born over here, you knew he was going to turn you in.

Bumming over to Denver, keeping out of trouble, staying straight an hour and a half. Pulling that crap in Ponca City, living *real* high with what's-her-name till the money ran out.

And every time you got somewhere, some place you liked a lot, something went wrong. Some of the time, it wasn't anyone else, it was something you messed up yourself.

Jack wondered how that happened. And how come even if you knew, it happened every fucking time?

◆ ◆ ◆

It got pretty easy when his eyes got used to the dark. He felt his way along the wall, cement block, cool and slightly damp. His fingers found familiar shapes. Cabinets or boxes, he couldn't tell which, apparitions in the underground night.

He knew he was walking downhill, the room getting narrow, the far wall closer all the time. He sensed something coming, backed off and stopped. Reached out and touched it, a cyclone fence.

He panicked a moment, sure the fence had trapped him, blocked his way out. Then, working his way around, he saw the fence butted against the two walls, continued down the room, with a narrow walkway in between.

What the hell was that for? You did fences *up*. You didn't do fences underground.

He didn't know the answer, didn't really care. The room went somewhere, it didn't go to Piggs.

◆　◆　◆

When he found where it went, he almost turned back. The dark room ended abruptly, in a crumbling brick wall. An iron ladder was imbedded in the brick. The ladder was rusty and the only way was up. When he touched the lower rung, it came off in his hand. Bricks tumbled to the floor. Something squealed and ran across his foot.

"*Shit,*" Jack said.

He looked up in the dark. Reached up and grabbed a rung. Jerked it hard and it didn't come off. Found the rung above that. A hand and then a foot. Pause, take a breath, take a step again.

His head hit something hard. He felt it, knew what it was. The cover to a mini-manhole, the thing the guy lifts up to shut your water off. He reached up and pushed. The cover wouldn't give. Jack stepped up another rung, put his shoulder in it and shoved. The third time it gave. Dirt tumbled down in his face. He closed his eyes, opened them again. He was fifteen feet from the far side of Wan's. Ortega was sitting on the steps, reading under a twenty-watt bulb. Humming to himself, smoking a cigarette. The night was hot, and the sky was full of stars...

TEN...

Jack pulled himself up, put the cover back, stirred the dirt around. Stood, and walked to Wan's. Ortega looked up and set down his magazine.

"I think they gonna kill you, Jack. Rhino says it'll be wors'n than that."

"I expect he's right."

"Rhino says he was you, he'd go to Delaware."

"Why up there?"

"'Cause Cat don't know where it is."

"I'll keep it in mind."

"I think the whales are against us," Ortega said. "I think there is evil in these great creatures we've yet to dream about."

"I never thought much about it."

"You look at a whale sometime. You look him right in the eye."

"I will," Jack said.

Ortega was reading *Discover* magazine. Ortega liked nature. Especially otters, animals that lived in the sea. Jack felt he was fifty, maybe eighty-six. His skin was the color of clay. Three-day beard. Never one or two. Wore those Pancho Villa outfits all the time. Wore them waiting tables at Wan's Far Eastern Bar & Restaurant.

When Jack first met Ortega, he was startled by his speech, which sounded like someone named Sven. He was born in Tuxpan, Mexico, and deserted as a child when his mother passed through Hope, North Dakota. Ortega was raised by friendly Swedes, and lived there until he was seventeen. Though he spoke very little greaser at all, he was fiercely loyal to his native Mexico, and hated all whites.

"What do you know about Chavez?" Jack said. "What kind of guy is he, what's he do?"

"Ricky Chavez."

"Big guy. Comes over here from San Antone."

"I know who he is, Jack. You don't have to tell me who he is."

"Okay, I won't."

"Good."

"Am I insulting you or what?"

"A white man's thinking, both these dudes are tacos, they gonna know each other, right? Am I right? Fuck you, pal."

Jack sat down on the steps. "What's the matter with you? You been drinking again?"

"We are all *borracho*. Read you fockin' Hemingway. It ees thees thing of the drink, *inglés.*"

"I feel I may have caught you in a bad frame of mind."

"This could be. You think they would put me in the pen if I killed Rhino?"

"I doubt it."

"Good. Then I will. Chavez owns a bank in San Antonio. Also one in Kerrville. He has about a billion acres near Carrizo Springs."

"Jesus. That explains the gold-toed boots."

"People of the Hispanic persuasion say a man like this has the *suerte*. Luck, good fortune."

"That's what people of the Anglo persuasion say, too."

Jack stood. "You going to do anything, you going to sit here all night?"

"Why don't you ask. Give me the courtesy of that."

"Okay. You think maybe I could use the car?"

"There is very little gas. I will hold you responsible, you run out and leave it somewhere."

"I wouldn't do that."

"Good. Because you have done this several times before."

"You people are a very suspicious race."

"I wonder where the *fock* we learn that?"

◆ ◆ ◆

It had to be well after four, closer to five. Clouds had swept in while he and Ortega talked. The stars had disappeared, and lightning flared off to the west. It wouldn't likely rain this time of the year, but anything could happen, even a wonder such as that.

Ortega kept his car beneath a live oak tree back of Wan's. The oak was a thick-boled giant that had managed, somehow, to avoid the lumber yard and the ravages of time. The tree was four hundred years old. Ortega's car was an '89 Plymouth, not nearly as sound as the tree.

The car smelled of garlic, beer and cigarettes. Hershey bars and sweat. The back seat was high with Budweiser cans. The front was an avalanche of *Pacific Otter* and *Nature Magazine*. The covers pictured happy seals, and ugly manatees.

Jack drove far enough to see down the street. Far enough to see the front of Piggs, close enough to Wan's to stay in the cover of the trees. He thought about the secret

53

that he'd found. A big empty room, a passage underground. He decided it must have been part of the seafood place that was there before Piggs. The only thing was, it seemed awful big for that. A hell of a cellar for a country restaurant.

Which didn't really have much to do with what might happen in the morning, which wasn't that far away now, an hour and a half. Wednesday was not his best day. The shit had hit the fan in Dallas on a Wednesday afternoon. They'd found him guilty—what else?—on a Wednesday, and bused him to Huntsville the Wednesday after that.

The best thing to do, Jack decided, was not even think about what might happen with Cecil or the Cat. The best thing to do was not wait around and find out. Take Ortega's car, drive it till it dropped. Catch a bus, haul ass completely out of state. Any state would be fine. As long as it wasn't Oklahoma, Texas, Colorado, Kansas or Arkansas.

The only thing was, he knew he couldn't run. He couldn't go no matter what they did. He could have before, but he couldn't do it now. Now, he had something going in his life, something worthwhile. He couldn't take off and leave Gloria behind. He would never, ever in his life, meet another woman like that.

❖ ❖ ❖

The parking lot was empty and that was fine with Jack. That meant Cecil had already left, along with Grape and Cat. Most of the girls didn't bring a car to work. Weirdos tended to hang around the lot. A guy or another girl would pick the girls up. Phylla's niece came and got her every night. They went by Gloria's place and dropped her off.

Jack didn't think she'd be upset. She wasn't like that. She'd told him no, but they could get around that. Go get some pie. Just ride around and talk. That's what he wanted anyway. Just to be with her, have some time to talk.

Someone picked up Minnie. Maggie pulled out in her car.

A Chevy stopped for Laura Licks.

Jack was concerned, but not much. Gloria always took her time. Getting to work and going back. Getting in her costume, taking it off again.

She might be late, but what she was not—and he wondered why it had even crossed his mind—what she was *not,* was out with that wetback fucking millionaire. She wasn't doing that. Chavez could buy a whole store full of cheap-ass flowers, she wouldn't be going out with him. Gloria had real values, Gloria was deeper than that.

Jack sat up straight. Gloria stepped out of Piggs. Nikes and jeans, black T-shirt. My, she looked fine, just as fine as she could be. Jack started up the Plymouth. It coughed and came to life.

A big car took the corner fast, headlights swept the empty street. The car swerved over to the curb, jerked to a halt. Someone got out.

Jack's heart stopped. Cecil said something to Gloria. Gloria stood there a minute, talking to Cecil, then got in the car. The door slammed shut, the Caddie took off, a lizard-green monster roaring through the night.

The street was still again. It was over quick as that. Jack could scarcely believe it had happened, but it did. The lightning flashed again, closer now, thunder rolling overhead. Two fat drops struck Juan Ortega's car.

Seeing her get in Cecil's Caddie shook him up, shook him up bad. He knew, though, knew in his heart, that Gloria's actions were mostly his fault. He had known this was so for some time, that this was a failing in himself, a failing he must now face squarely, bring up to the light. He had been too gentle, too easy, he had not asserted himself. He vowed that he would start doing that. Gloria had to quit stalling, had to let him take her out. They would never get anywhere until she did that. Then, they would get a lot closer, get to know each other well. They could talk about the future, make plans to settle down. Jack wished there was some other way, some way besides the dating part, which was such a fucking hassle every time, but he didn't see how he could get around that...

ELEVEN...

She wasn't real mad. Wasn't real happy, either, sitting in back of the green Cadillac with Cecil R. Dupree. Cecil, absolutely gross, straw hat and overalls, not even wearing a shirt, for Christ sake, white socks and Li'l Abner shoes. Hoping, Gloria and everybody knew, that some poor jerk would take him for a rube. Say something to him so Cecil could have Cat pound him into mush. Or if the guy wasn't too big, do the job himself.

It happened now and then, on the street or in a store. It happened in Austin, Waco or Dallas somewhere. Where it never happened was in a Mexican Wells, because everybody knew better there.

"This is real good," Cecil said, "this is sure fine. You and me are busy all the time, we never get a chance to talk."

"I don't guess we do," Gloria said.

"I was just thinking, Gloria and me, we don't get a chance to talk. What I ought to do, I ought to give her a ride sometime, we could have the time to talk."

"It's very nice of you, Mr. Dupree, you didn't have to do that."

"Course I didn't, I wanted to. And Lord, not *Mister* Dupree." Cecil gave a little laugh. "I feel old, a young lady calls me that. 'Mister,' is something you don't want to hear, you get as old as me."

"Oh, I don't think I could."

"Do what?"

"Call you that. I feel it would be a presumption on my part, me being in your employment and all."

"Well as your employ*er,* I say it's Cecil, I say it's all right."

"If you say so."

"Well I do."

"All right."

"Say it."

"Do what?"

"Say it. Say 'Cecil.'"

"You mean, just come out and say it? Nothing else with it, just by itself?"

"Just say it."

"All by itself."

"Jesus Christ, all by itself'd be fine."

"Cecil."

"What?"

"Cecil."

"Now see, that sounds real nice. And you are not presuming a thing, all right? I assure you of that."

Cecil assured her. A pat on the knee, a tiny little squeeze an inch or so above that.

Oh shit, here we go, Gloria said to herself, none of this coming as any big surprise, a road she'd been down once or twice before. A guy runs a club, runs a place like Piggs, he figures ladies of the unclad persuasion are inventory,

like peanuts and beer. You take a little sample now and
then, make sure it's all right.

Cecil hadn't ever hit on his girls. If he had, Gloria would
know in about a minute flat. Which didn't mean he wasn't
starting now. Guys like Cecil, he was halfway done. One
little feelie, that was the foreplay, that was romance. Onto
the good part, *bingo!* Roll on off and take a nap. It is plain
irritating, she thought, that I got to be first. How about
Laura and Maggie, why's he got to start with me?

There was no way out, she knew that. Jump out the
door, Cecil would get her right back. Gloria Mundi, both
legs broken, crawling down the road. Back in the car, Cat
Eye and Grape, putting on a splint, Cecil feeling her up
again.

◆ ◆ ◆

Cat Eye was driving, Cat Eye who scared her half to
death, a mean-ass grizzly with a minus IQ, the wheel buried somewhere in his lap. Grape there with him, squeezed
in somewhere, crushed against the door.

The AC was high as it would go, cold enough to freeze
an Eskimo. Not high enough, in Gloria's mind, to mask
the ghastly essence, the stink and the stench, that hung
in heavy layers in the car. All it did was make the Frito
farts and the taco breath, the belches and the sweats, the
day-old doughnuts and cigarette butts, smell cold.

Jack McCooly had told her once: "Gangsters smell
worse than anyone else. *The Learning Channel* did a whole
show on it, that's a scientific fact."

And Gloria thought: Jack McCooly doesn't have a lot
of sense, but he is dead-on right about that.

◆ ◆ ◆

The rain passed quickly, leaving scarcely any mark behind, moving on south to disappoint a hundred Texas towns. The night began to fade, giving way to pale bands of lavender, peach and dirty gray, worn and tattered colors, washed too many times, left out to dry in the hot and unforgiving summer day.

A traffic light blinked on Crockett and Main. Cat Eye ran it, drove through town in a minute and a half. Dark farm houses after that, the single harsh glare of a 7-Eleven store. Two more miles down the empty highway. Cat Eye made a hard left, stopped too fast, gravel snapped beneath the tires. And, for an instant, the headlights swept across a sign, hanging, dangling at a tilt, battered, sun-peeled, weathered and cracked, rusted and pocked by shooters passing by, the words so faded they might have been purple, crimson or black. The sign, if you took the time to read it, said:

BATTLE OF BRITUN
FAMILY FUN PARK

A gate blocked the way. Cecil leaned up and said, "Grape, get out and get that."

"Now you don't need to," Gloria said, "I can do it just fine—"

Popped the door and slid out fast, one foot quickly on the ground. Cecil stretched out a hillbilly hand, gently pulled her back.

"Hey, I won't have that. I don't see a lady home, leave her walking in the dark."

His fingers felt cold and the dark was just fine.

"It isn't any trouble, I do it all the time."

"We haven't had a chance to talk."

"We ought to do that. We ought to set a time."

"Right now's just fine for me."

"It is awful late, all right?"
"It's awful early's what it is. You got any coffee up at your place?"
"I am real tired, Mr. Dupree."
"Cecil."
"What?"
"You were going to call me Cecil. We talked about that. I said, you don't have to call me Mr. Dupree. You said, all right, that'll be fine."
"It is awful early, *Cecil,* could we do it some other time? Don't take offense, I am simply too tired."
"You'll feel better," Cecil said, "you get off your feet a while. The dance is a demanding profession, you don't have to tell me that. I've known dancers all my life. I know how much you're giving of yourself."
She didn't look at him, didn't try again. Knew there wasn't any use in that. The way his words came out said Cecil was tired of being nice. Tired of acting like someone had a say but him.
She stepped out on the road. The days were too hot to let the night cool down. After the car, the hot smelled clean. Dry yellow grass, the dusty scent of summer trees.
Cat Eye turned the lights off. Grape and the Cat stayed in the car. The stock gate was rusty metal pipe that could swing open wide to let a cattle truck in. There weren't any cattle inside, and the gate was secondhand.
She opened the padlock and slid off the chain.
"Now this is interesting," Cecil said. "I been by your place a hundred times, but I never been in."
"Isn't much left for anyone to see," Gloria said, and walked off toward the trees.

◆ ◆ ◆

He walked behind her through the pale morning light, the day still cloaked in muted shades of night, bleak enough still through the stand of ancient oaks to hide a dark array of ghosts. He knew they were there, an angle and a shape, nothing real clear. Dim and blurry phantoms, lost and indistinct, lost until one of them hit him in the head.

"Whoa!" Cecil said, threw up his hands, touched cold metal and ducked beneath a wing. Passed on quickly, kept the girl in sight. Didn't know what he'd nearly hit. Didn't know the ghost was a Hawker Hurricane, didn't know its foe, twenty yards ahead, was a riddled Messerschmitt, the pilot a blur under faded plexiglass, dying, now, or already dead. Didn't know the pilot had served once before, served in the window of Flicker's Men's Store.

Didn't know the Mustang he passed, didn't know a Storch. Didn't know a Stuka in desert coloration. Knew, though, it used to be a snow cone stand.

Cecil didn't know and didn't care. He'd passed the place before, scarcely glanced at the hollow relics then. Knew it had closed down many years before. Knew, later, that one of his dancers lived there, learned who it was when Gloria Mundi caught his eye.

Cecil Dupree didn't waste a lot of time on anything that didn't have tits, anything without a dollar sign. Didn't care what happened outside the walls of Piggs. Didn't read the papers, didn't keep up with world events.

He knew, though, that Gloria Mundi was a honey and a half, that she had a certain something the other girls lacked. He didn't know what, but he meant to find out. And, if he had to follow that fine-looking ass through a maze of rusty scrap, well he could handle that.

As long as she didn't put him off. Mess around yakking an hour and a half, all the preliminary shit a woman had to do before she quit. Cecil hated that. Hated walking through the fucking woods. Hated being outdoors every-where you looked.

He was walking so close he nearly ran her down. "Hey, whoa," he said, grabbing her shoulders tight, "what we stopping for, babe?"

Gloria gave him a weary look. "We're here, Mr. Dupree. This is where I live."

"Where," Cecil said, "I don't see a thing." He made a big deal out of stomping around, shading his brow, peering like an Indian through the stand of trees. "You live in a hole, got a tepee somewhere?"

"Up there."

"Up where?"

"Up there, Mr. Dupree."

"I asked you to call me Cec—Holy shit, you're kidding, right? Doesn't anybody live up there."

"Well I'm anybody, I take offense to that."

"You're overly sensitive, anyone ever tell you that?" Cecil peered up again. "Maybe no one mentioned it before, this isn't your ordinary house."

"I'm not a ordinary person, I don't pretend to be."

That is the goddamn truth, Cecil thought, staring at the thing, looking straight up, looking at it perched there, thirty, forty feet up in the big oak tree, blocking out every-thing, blocking out the whole fucking sky. How it got up there was something else again, but it was there, all right, a really big mother, bigger than the relics on the ground, just hanging in the branches like it *grew* right there, and Cecil knew it hadn't done that, knew someone put it there.

"Well, it is something to see, I got to say that," Cecil said, because he couldn't think of anything else. "Say, am I still going to get a drink?"

"I said coffee, don't be expecting something else."

"Coffee's fine. I don't suppose you got a doughnut too?"

"No," she said, "I don't suppose I do."

"No problem," Cecil said, and anyone who knew him knew that wasn't so, knew he had doughnuts, coffee, scrambled eggs and bacon, every morning at nine.
It was light enough to see him well now. She looked to the side, didn't look him in the face. It was awkward to keep doing that, worse if you didn't even try. Cecil looked bad. Cecil looked bad all the time. He might, though, look a little worse, she decided, in the pale morning lavender light.

"I don't mean to be blunt," she told him, "don't take what I'm saying like that. What I'm saying is, I don't have company a lot, Mr. Dupr—Cecil. Nothing personal, it's just the way I am. In the entertainment field you're with people all the time, I don't have to tell you that. I don't get a lot of time to myself. When I do, it is precious to me, and I don't care to share it with anyone else. So how long you think this talking's going to take?"

Cecil blinked. "Hell, I don't know how long we're going to talk, I'm hoping to get it done quick."

"I hope I don't misunderstand that."

"I surely hope you don't, I can't imagine any reason that you would. What I was thinking, we could have that coffee, maybe you could be polite. I'm sure you had manners one time, I'm sure your mother said treat people nice. I think we could get to know one another, get to be friends, see what happens after tha—"

Cecil stopped. Gloria was gone. She'd walked away and simply disappeared. Cecil looked behind him, turned and looked ahead. Stepped around a big live oak that was broad as he was tall. Scrap wood rungs had been nailed to the trunk, like a little kid had put them there. Stepping back then, squinting through the branches, through the half light, he saw her there, climbing straight up.

"Oh Jesus," Cecil said. He felt a little knot in his belly, felt a little something in his throat. The tree seemed to

lean, seemed to waver, seemed to sway. Cecil wasn't scared
of anything at all. Cecil wasn't even scared of God. He was
scared to even think about climbing up a tree. And, he
thought, if anyone knew that, anyone at Piggs, Cat Eye or
Grape or anyone at all...
He took a deep breath. Kept his eye steady on the
trunk. Didn't look up, didn't look down. Slid one hand up
the tree, clutched one rung and then the next. Slid one leg
and then another after that. Hugged the tree hard, learned
trees were big, learned trees were sound. Learned, if you
didn't let go, the tree would be your friend.
Stopped once. Wiped off the sweat with his sleeve, keeping both hands on the tree. Risked a glance up, knew, at
once, this was the wrong thing to do. Saw where he was,
saw the trees and the sky. Knew he was high enough to
die. Knew he was——
*"THIS IS YOUR JU 52 JUNKERS AIRPLANE,
THE WORKHORSE OF THE GERMAN AIR
FORCE..."*
The loudspeaker blared. Fifty-two strings of Christ-
mas tree lights started blinking overhead. Cecil nearly
lost it, Cecil hugged the tree for dear life.
*"...WHAT MANY OF YOU MAY NOT KNOW IS AN
EARLY VERSION OF THIS CELEBRATED CRAFT*
Grrrrrrk-hissssh! *TOOK WING IN 1930. AFTER THAT
IT WENT THROUGH MANY ALTERATIONS IN-
CLUDING PASSENGER AIRPLANE, TRANSPORT
AND BOMBER, BECOMING, AS MANY OF YOU
KNOW, ONE OF* Skkkkkrreeeek *THE MOST FAMOUS
AIRCRAFT OF ALL TIME. THE PLANE YOU SEE
HERE WAS FIRST BUILT AT THE JUNKERS
FLUGDZENG UND MOTERENWERKE AG. RIGHT
BEFORE THE WAR, THE g3e BOMBER TYPES
WERE ROLLING OUT OF FACTORIES AT DESSAU
AND BERNBERG. POWERED BY* Shrrriiik—hrrrrrr!

THREE BMW 132T DASH TWO RADIAL ENGINES, THE PLANE ATTAINED A MAXIMUM SPEED OF THREE-OH-FIVE KILOMETRES PER HOUR, WITH A RANGE OF—Griiiiik-griiik!

"Sorry 'bout that," Gloria said, poking her head out an open port above. "Can't ever get that tape to go anywhere but high. Shoot, I guess you noticed that. You all right, Mr. Dupree? You coming up or what?"

TWELVE...

. . .I can tell you there's people who'll say it right out, I mean, even if they're tryin' to be polite, you know what I mean? Someone wouldn't incite your feelings for anything at all like Maggie Thatch whom I'm very close to? Well you'd think, until it all comes out. We are in the middle of a TV show, that *Discovery* thing about gnus? She hits that MUTE and says, Gloria Jean, you're a absolute nut, you are crazy as shit, girlfriend. Isn't anyone mentally right living in a German warplane. Isn't any fucking *Germans* doin' that. They're living in houses like everybody else.

"Well I am taken aback. I tell her, look, it is not for everyone, it is just fine for *me*. I don't tell you not to live in the Lamprey Motel, which I wouldn't *drive* by, hon, for fear of a social disease. Well she didn't take well to that, things haven't been right between us since.

"See, I grew up in this thing, okay? Lord, I know that spiel by heart. Every time I hear Daddy talk I like to bust out crying but I haven't got the heart to take him off.

"The place went busted when I was thirteen, just after Mama died, and that flat finished Daddy off. He took to drink soon after and I went to live with Aunt Brill. I don't guess I'd of ever come back if he hadn't passed on. I needed a place real bad, or you wouldn't *see* this girl in Mexican Wells, I'd be somewhere they got a streetlight. I hope you're not looking for sugar or cream, I don't serve either one."

"Black's the way I like it," Cecil said, "that's fine."

It wasn't, it was bad. Instant, not even hot, not even stirred, little black crystals floating on top. He'd watched her make it, knew what he'd get. Watched her in the very tight kitchen up between the wings. Hot plate, counter and a sink, little tiny fridge. Not a whole lot, but there was hardly room for that.

Jesus Christ, hardly room for anything, as far as he could tell. He wondered how people got about. Wondered if Germans were smaller than anyone else. It was kind of like the tunnels you used to crawl in, write dirty stuff on the walls. Only these walls were corrugated tin. The walls, the floors, inside the plane and out. The whole thing astonished Cecil. And, at the same time, made him feel at home. This was the very same stuff they'd used to build Piggs. Why, he could build a bomber himself if he ever wanted to.

There were little canvas seats, folded up right against the wall. You wanted to sit, you folded one down. Gloria had put little cushions down, souvenirs from several Western states. Good idea, Cecil thought. A lot of Germans had sat in those seats, and they weren't exactly clean.

◆ ◆ ◆

Cecil sat and watched. Watched that tight little ass when she bent for something low. Watched how the T-shirt bared her belly button when she reached for something high. Knew he was right, knew the climb was worth the trip. Man, he loved to see her dressed. He wanted her

68

just like this. Maybe she had some other clothes, women always did. Maybe he could see her in a lot of different stuff.

"—I used to take cream and sugar both, I mean *spoonfuls,* I don't mean a little bit, you know what that *does* to the body tissue, well I quit that. You want to keep dancin' you can't even look at something's got sugar or fat—"

Gloria stopped, felt her face flush. Saw him looking at her, tried to look at something else.

"I am babbling like a brook, you know what? I don't ever do that. I'm a little hot, that fan's not working just right."

"Fan's just fine," Cecil said. "What you're doing, hon, you're running kinda scared."

Gloria nearly dropped her cup. "Just what do you mean by that? What have I got to be scared about, Mr. Dupree?"

"I guess you'd know as well as me."

"I don't guess I would."

Cecil had to grin. He knew scared when he saw it. She sat on a stool, sat with her knees real tight. Holding the saucer on her knees, looking at him now like he'd caught her in his headlights, caught her in the road.

"You didn't want me comin' up here, you're madder'n hell about that. You tried being nasty, that didn't work, so you start running off at the mouth. Now that is a normal behavior, that and pissin' in your pants. What you're thinking, you're thinking, is he going to make me fuck him or not? That's what I came for, you know that as well as me, that's why I got you in the car."

"Well are you?"

"I was. That was my intention. I might not do it now."

"Why not? I mean, I'm grateful for your hesitation, I appreciate that."

"I used to do crazy shit, you know? Stuff a kid'll do, like you see this Mes'can walking, you *know* you're goin' to run the sucker down. Haven't got any damn reason, okay? You just flat gotta run him down. Another thing is, take something off a fella, something you don't even need. He's maybe got a dollar, he's got a fuckin' comb. Burn some bozo's trailer down. Used to do that all the time. You don't even know the guy, you burn his trailer down.

"See that's growing up. You get to be a adult person, you quit doing shit like that, you start using your head. You say, Cecil, Cecil Dupree, you got a choice. You can do what you want, you can do anything you like, can't anyone can stop you doing that. You can screw this very lovely person all night, you don't even gotta ask. You get tired of that you can burn her fucking airplane down.

"You don't want to do that, you can give her a puppy. Give her a kitty cat. Give her a trip to Paris, France. You don't have to do none of the above, you don't have to do anything at all. You see what I'm saying? You get to be Cecil Dupree, it's just as big a kick *not* to do something as it is. Hey, I never get into personal stuff, I think I'm kinda taken with you."

"Sometimes it helps to open up and share," Gloria said. "I can understand that..."

"Huh-unh. Don't. Do not ever mess with me, Gloria. Do not ever tell me shit you think I want to hear."

Gloria's heart nearly stopped. He didn't raise his voice, didn't glare, didn't stare, didn't show her anything at all. What happened, happened in his face, the thing that was there getting dark and darker still, getting dark as liver, getting close to black.

Cecil got up. Put down his cup.

"Don't tell those cunts at Piggs I was here. Don't fuck anyone, don't go out of town. I am declaring my affection for you, Gloria, you understand that? This is a serious matter to me. If you got any smarts at all, you'll respect my feelings, okay? And get some real coffee, grind the beans yourself. Find a place to live. Cecil Dupree don't go with some broad, you gotta climb a fucking tree…"

THIRTEEN...

The sun flared over the trees, howling in a nuclear rage, incandescent anger in its single flaming eye, simmering and seething, pissed at everyone. Ate up the night, sucked the morning dry. Chewed up a dawn in Tennessee, hawked it back up, spit it on southern Arkansas. Loosed all its fury on Texas, determined to burn the state down this time, starting with Mexican Wells...

◆ ◆ ◆

Cecil stomped out in the sun, neck burning up, over-alls sticking to his knees. Gut still churning from climb-ing down the tree. Hoppers jumped ahead. Gnats came out and headed for his nose. Cecil got in the car and said, "Get the hell out of here, Cat."

"Hey, what happened," Grape said, "you get any, man?"

"Shut the fuck up," Cecil said.

Grape was much smarter than Cat, but Grape had been napping and didn't see Cecil stomping through the weeds, wading through the wrecks, didn't know what was going on, got a look at Cecil's face half a second late. Sat back, shut up, didn't say a word after that.

The ride back to Piggs was very quiet. Cat Eye thought about a pie. A chocolate or a peach. Grape thought about a drink. Cecil thought about Gloria Mundi. Thought about her in a going-out dress, a dress that fits good, like you see in a ladies' magazine. Thought about her in an apron, cooking something nice. Remembered her coffee, decided to think of something else.

What he thought about most, was whether he ought to be doing this at all. Messing with the help is no good. Even if you own the place, you're asking for trouble right off. The guy runs the bar, he's going to steal a little more. Even the guy sweeps up, he's sore because everybody else is sore, too.

The dancers, Jesus, that's the worst of all. A person of the stripper persuasion is strung out to start. Piss 'em off, and they'll drive you fucking nuts.

Gloria Mundi, Cecil thinks, is a bad idea. Slap her around, do what you want to do. Do that, she's out the door fast. Wait her out, be nice, she maybe comes around. Then what? Then you got to buy her shit, take her into town.

Whatever you do, it'll turn out wrong. Cecil knows that, he's done it all before. He also knows he is wasting time thinking about it, he knows he's going to do it all again.

◆ ◆ ◆

Cecil is sitting in the back. Cat Eye's driving, Grape is in the front. Cecil looks at the back of Cat's head. He looks at the back of Cat's head maybe five, six times a day. Cat's neck is very thick. It has seven folds of fat. Cat shaves his head close, right down to the skin. And even if there isn't any hair up there, Cat has dandruff anyway. Little flakes falling on his shirt, on the seat behind his back. Cecil's used to that, he sees it all the time. But this is not an ordinary day. It's six in the morning, he's been up all night. He didn't get laid, all he did was climb a tree. His face is on fire. His face gets worse when he's mad. It burns like someone's dropping kitchen matches on his skin.

I feel like shit, I gotta sit and look at that, Cecil thinks, I gotta look at Cat's head.

"Stop," Cecil says, poking Cat in the back, "stop the fucking car. Stop at the 7-Eleven store."

"Gotcha," Cat says.

The store is maybe half a mile away. Cat pulls in. The store is bright with cold fluorescent light. A million crickets are bouncing off the windows outside.

Grape turns around. "What you need, Cecil, what you want me to get?"

"I don't want you to do nothing," Cecil says. "Cat, go in the store. Get some Head 'n Shoulders. Get me a Coke. Get me a Snickers, better make it two."

"I'd like some Fritos," Grape says. "See if they got a Big Red."

"Get it yourself," Cecil says, "don't be asking him. I don't remember he's in your employ, I think he works for me."

"Right," Grape says, and doesn't look at Cecil again.

Cecil gets out. The windows on the Caddie are tinted, and he squints in the sudden morning light. Reaches in the pocket of his overalls, can't find his shades. He can smell the coffee they're making inside. Maybe he'll have a coffee too. Maybe get a doughnut. You can get a good doughnut or a roll, you get there early before they're all gone.

Two little black kids are making wide circles on the drive, running over crickets with their bikes. They are

75

seven or eight, maybe thirteen. Cecil can't tell. Nigger-rap T-shirts, worn-out jeans. Brand new basketball shoes, bigger than either kid's head. When the tires get a cricket, they make an awful sound.

Cat Eye comes out. He's chewing on a doughnut, sugar all over his mouth.

"They didn't have a Snickers," Cat says, "I had to get a Mars."

"I don't want a Mars, I want a Snickers," Cecil says.

"They didn't have none."

"You didn't look."

"They hadda Milky Way and Mars, that's all they got."

"They got a Hershey with nuts, why'nt you get that?"

"You said a Snickers. You said, get me a Snickers and a Coke."

"Fuck it, gimme that."

Cecil takes the paper sack. Opens up his Coke, looks at his Mars. Hands the Head 'n Shoulders to Cat. "Go over there. They got a hose by the tanks. Shampoo your head."

"Huh?" Cat Eye looks blank. "What for?"

"Do it. Do it right now. You're making me fucking sick."

Cat Eye doesn't argue. Cat knows better than that. He doesn't tell Cecil you don't shampoo if you don't have hair. Even if you did, you didn't do it at the 7-Eleven store.

He takes off his shirt and lays it on the hood. Walks over to the gas tanks, turns on the hose. Takes the top off the shampoo.

The young kid running the store looks out. Sees Cecil and the Cat. Sees the lizard-green Cadillac. Decides he doesn't care to get into that.

Cecil drinks his Coke. Doesn't like the Mars. Likes the nuts fine, doesn't like white stuff inside.

One of the kids has a Cowboys gimme-cap, bill turned to the back.

"Why he doin' that," he asks Cecil. "How come he washin' his head?"

""Cause he wants to," Cecil says.

"Man hadn't got any hair."

"Won't do any good," the other kid says, "man hasn't got any hair."

The kids go *huk-huk-huk!* Cover up their mouths to hold the giggles back. Pedal in circles round Cecil, laughing and looking at Cat.

"Stop it," Cecil said, "quit doing that."

"Doin' what?"

"Running over bugs."

"Ain't your bugs, man."

"You listening, kid? Don't squash the bugs. I don't like to hear you squashing bugs."

The first kid grins at his friend. "Better not squish no bugs. Lone don't like you squishin' bugs."

The other kid laughs.

Cecil says, "What? What'd you say to me?"

The kid's not dumb. The kid pedals quickly away, making a bigger circle with his friend.

"Called you Lone," says the friend. "Got you a mask and all, you the Lone Ranger, man."

"Where you Indian, where Tonto, man?"

"Tonto, he givin' hisself a *sham*-poo."

"Shit. Tonto ain't got any hair, can't get a *sham*-poo, man don't got any hair."

"Where your horse, man? Where Silver at, he waitin' in the car?"

The kids laugh and howl. They make big circles and run over crickets. *Squish-squash-squish.*

"Gimme the keys," Cecil says.

"What for?" Grape says.

"Gimme the *keys,* Grape."

Cecil holds out his hand and snatches the keys. Walks around and opens the trunk. Paws through beer cans and sacks, finds the Winchester, the 12-gauge pump.

"Cecil, that ain't a good idea."

"Get in the car. Get Cat, get him in the back."

"What I'd like you to do, I'd like you to think about this."

"I already did," Cecil says, racking a shell in the chamber, *snack-snick!* "Killing the poor is a blessing, Grape. What kinda life these little bastards gonna have, you ever think about that?"

"Yeah, but—"

"Going to grow up and have *more* little kids, that's what. Little assholes'll be running over bugs."

Cecil raises the weapon and fires. The butt slams into his shoulder, the barrel jerks up into the air. Cartons of Cokes are stacked in front of the store. The cartons explode in a hail of foam and glass.

The kids scream and howl, duck their heads and pedal for their lives. Cecil stands behind his car, coolly blasting one load and then another down the street. He fires until every shell is gone, until the kids are out of sight.

The boy in the 7-Eleven is down behind the counter on the floor. Cat's eyes are full of shampoo, he can't see a thing. He can hear someone shooting, he doesn't know what.

"Holy shit," Grape says, sitting in the car. He looks straight ahead, he doesn't look back. If Cecil has shot two little black boys, he doesn't want to know about that. He needed a drink half an hour ago, and he really needs it now...

FOURTEEN...

Jack sat in the Yak.

Small explosions of fierce morning light pierced the thick green canopy above. One caught Jack, struck him dead center, stung him in the eye. "Thanks," Jack said, "I guess I needed that."

He was grateful for the help. He'd nodded off again for a minute and a half. He was tired, he was hot and he needed to pee. Sitting up straight, he squinted at the big German plane in the live oak tree.

He had spent a lot of mornings in old aircraft of the Allied and enemy persuasion, waiting for the instant, waiting for the magic moment she'd appear. He had left his mark in mad dog Messerschmitts, Zeros and P-38s. Fat-bellied Wildcats, Mustangs and Spits. Mac sacks, Pepsi cans and chicken buckets littered the cockpits of ancient airplanes. Twice—and he wasn't proud of this— he'd left peculiar stains.

It was always the same. No matter when she got in, two o'clock or four, she'd open the door behind the rusty, corrugated wing, open the door and just stand there awhile before she turned in. Stand there, dry her hair and yawn, watching the sun come yellow through the trees. And the fine thing was, the thing that made Jack's heart swell, was she didn't wear anything dirty, something short and black like you see in a girlie magazine. She wore a long nightgown that came below her knees, a nightie with Mickeys and Minnies all over, like a little kid'd do. And even if Jack was freezing cold, or broiling in sweat like he was doing now, he never thought about leaving, not till he saw her up there. Not till the warm and loving thoughts had time to settle down inside his head.

This time, though, there wasn't any love up there, there was sorrow and murder in his head. Sorrow for himself, and murder for Cecil R. Dupree, who was up there with her where he, Jack, had never been. Sorrow and shame, because he knew what he ought to do was climb up and kill him, kill the sorry bastard any way he could. Climb up and do it, not even think about what might happen after that.

What he did wasn't anything at all, because Huntsville had sucked all the killer part out, drained him and left him with a hole in his belly and a fright in his soul. The mean was still in him, he could feel it in there, mean left over from the Choctaw-Irish Oklahoma kid, from the man he became after that. It was there, but he just couldn't reach it anymore.

❖ ❖ ❖

A big crow landed on the plane's right wing. Then another, and another after that. They squawked and they strutted, and poked each other with their bills. Jack knew crows were real smart. Grandpa Rait had told him so, when they sat on the bank at Shallow Creek, fishing for crappie and cat. Grandpa Rait was mostly full of shit, but he knew about crows, there wasn't any bull in that.

The door opened up and the crows scattered quick. It wasn't Gloria, it was Cecil R. Dupree. Jack's heart skipped a beat. The ugly flush across Cecil's face was darker than Jack had ever seen. His eyes were little cuts, his mouth was thin and mean. Muttering, talking to himself, Cecil made his way down the tree. Missed a few slats, nearly fell twice, stomped through the woods and headed toward the road.

Jack watched until Cecil was out sight. Looked up at the plane, looked a second too late. The door slammed shut and she was gone.

What he could do, he could go up there, he could climb up and talk. She was all distraught, she'd welcome some comfort right now. And, sorrow and anger and pissed off aside, what he knew, what he knew was surely true, was she'd brought Cecil there against her will. Nothing had happened up there, Cecil's face told him that. That mark was as good as those mood rings the stores used to sell. If Cecil'd done her, he'd be kind of coral, light strawberry, he wouldn't be black. Jack had seen him black once or twice, and he knew what that was like.

Go up and see her then, lay it all out, like he should have done before. Tell her they had to start dating or they'd never get close. She simply had to understand that. How love was a two-way street, he couldn't do it all alone.

Another thing he'd tell her, which would show her how he felt, was he'd stay there at Piggs. Even if Cat half killed him, he wouldn't run off, he wouldn't go away. If she'd have him, if they'd go out now and then for pie, if she'd let love try and have its way, he'd put up with anything else. He thought that'd do it. If that didn't work, then nothing else would.

Out of the Yak, then, onto the ground. Stretched for a minute to get the kinks out. Started for the ladder—stopped, hesitated. Made himself try again.

Halfway there, and he heard a branch snap, heard it real close, froze in his tracks behind a tree.

The sound came again. A cough, then another. Someone else was in the woods, someone close by. Someone—

Cecil! Oh Jesus, Cecil hasn't left, he's coming back now!

Jack drew a breath, caught a blur of motion to his right. Five, six yards off in the trees. Past the red fighter without a tail. He turned his head slowly, an inch at a time. The figure moved again. Out in the open, away from the trees.

Jack stared. It wasn't Cecil, it was somebody else. It was that big Mex, fucking Ricky Chavez, with the solid gold buckle on his belt. Standing there with a dozen wilted roses, looking up sadly at Gloria's tree.

"Godamn it," Jack said to himself, "these people got to stop, I cannot keep putting up with this..."

❖ ❖ ❖

It was way past seven when he drove Ortega's car back and parked beneath the live oak tree. Cecil's car was back in Cecil's spot, in the alley next to Piggs. They were all asleep, then. Cecil up there in his room, Cat on his cot behind the stairs. Jack knew for sure that he slept with his eyes wide open, a sight fairly frightening to see. Conscious, or in a deep coma—either state was fine with him.

Jack settled down in the back room at Wan's, back behind cartons of toilet paper, soy sauce, chiles, and great tins of MSG. It was too late to try and go to bed. He could lie down and rest, though, make sure he didn't go to sleep.

For some peculiar reason, he felt unusually calm, almost at ease, and wondered just how that could be. In a couple of hours, someone would hurt him real bad. Cecil wouldn't let Cat kill him. Help was too hard to get in Mexican Wells. Almost anyone could do a lot better than Piggs. Cat wouldn't kill him, then—but whatever he did, it wouldn't feel good.

"Jhack, what the fock you doin' here, mahn? I t'ink you are gone, I never be seein' you again."

"Well I'm here," Jack said, "if that's all right with you."

"Hey, is aw'right wi' me, hah? I am t'inking, though, you pretty crazy in the head, Jhack. I t'ink you smarter than dat."

"Well I'm not, so just shut up about it, okay?"

"Hokay, Jhack."

"Hokay your fuckin' self. Just leave me alone, I gotta get some rest."

Ahmed was in the far corner somewhere, behind the sacks of rice. Rice felt a lot like sand, he'd told Jack, it even felt better sometimes.

"Why you be comin' back, mahn? These not a good idea, I know dat…"

"I love it here, okay? How could you ask for a better place than this? Good bed, good pay. Some asshole from overseas talking all the time. All the Chink food you can eat. What else could a guy want besides that?"

"Hokay, Jhack."

"Shut up, you said that. Don't go saying it again."

"Hey, Jhack."

"What?"

"I know these guy one time, he has got a place sout' of Baghdad? Wat these guy is doin, he is tired of t'inkin' all da time. All the time he gotta t'ink of ever t'ing hisself. So wat he do, he say, 'Allah, you do the t'inkin' I am no t'inkin' anymore.' So he don', hokay? He start off walkin', run into a wall. Get up, start walkin' somewhere else. Maybe a fruit or somet'in fall outa tree, he gonna eat dat. Maybe it rain sometime, he gonna get a drink. He walk into a shop, right through da glass, knock ever' t'ing down. Someone hit these guy, knock him in da head. He don' care, he get up and go again..."

"Jesus, is there a point to this or what?"

"I don' t'ink so, Jhack."

"Now how did I know that? Shut up, don't you tell me nothing, you hear?"

Jack waited, waited for Ahmed to mouth off again because Ahmed always did. He hated to sleep in the storeroom. Not just because of Ahmed, because of the smell. The smell was the same as the storeroom in Huntsville prison—cardboard, potatoes, lettuce and tomatoes. Flour, sugar, things in boxes and cans.

People didn't know cans smelled. You get enough cans stacked up, they've got a certain smell. They don't smell like anything but cans.

Color was the other thing that stuck in his head. White shirt and pants if you were good. Pea-green if a man was truly bad. Bad guys took great pride in their greens. Big black dudes with rheumy eyes. Little guys with killer eyes from "K" Wing, where the Mexican Mafia was king. Skinhead whites from the Aryan Brotherhood. The whites, he recalled, were either pole-thin or hog fat, nothing in between.

Everything around you was painted in pale dirty colors that didn't have a name. No purples, no yellows, no reds.

The first thing he did when they let him out was buy a bright red shirt and yellow pants. You could always spot a con who'd just come out. He looked like a fucking rainbow for a while.

He didn't mean to sleep but he did. He was thinking about the day "C" Wing had gotten out of hand, and the guards had tossed in a gas grenade. He took that thought into a dream, heard the quick explosion, saw the baby-shit yellow cloud of smoke come at him, felt his eyes and his skin and the inside of his nose begin to burn...

...That dream flipped into another, this one featuring Billy Joe Weal, a lifer Jack had met in the yard at one time. Billy, who was just twenty-two, had robbed a convenience store, shot the clerk dead, and run off with eighteen dollars and thirty-nine cents. An Oklahoma boy of the skinhead persuasion, Billy had tattoos up and down his arms of swastikas, eagles, daggers and the like. And, across his chest, the words **HI, HITLER!** in bold Gothic script.

No one, not even his Aryan brothers, had the nerve to tell him it wasn't quite right. Billy was not only dumb, he was also a mean little shit...

...And, as the tar on the roof began to boil, and the room down below was hot enough to bake a brick, Ahmed cried out in his sleep, a long Iraqi curse that hopped into Jack's dream. The words began to spill out of Billy Joe Weal, and somehow seemed to make sense...

15 FIFTEEN...

Hutt Kenny drove his rental Buick through Martindale, Fentris, Prairie View and Luling, turned off 80 onto Interstate 10. Ten went straight through Houston, Beaumont, Baton Rouge, and finally down to New Orleans. Something close to five hundred miles and nothing in between that Kenny cared to see. What he wanted to see was the Louisiana line. That, and a girl on Chartres Street named Jill. Jill looked a lot like Gloria whatsit, that knockout dancer at Piggs. Okay, she didn't, but she looked pretty good, you didn't see her in the light.

Just thinking about Texas, Piggs, and fucking Zorro the Hick, made Kenny start to boil. The guy was a loony, a nut. Smart, you got to say that, but crazy as shit. As crazy as Ambrose Junior, only Junior wasn't smart. The old man, now, there's a guy that's smart. Only Junior was running the show now, and he's the guy Kenny had to call. Call up and tell him what Cecil said, how he wouldn't go along. Even if you left out all the bad parts, Junior would blow his stack.

And that was something scary to see. A guy is maybe dumb, he can still put a hole in your head, it doesn't take smarts to do that.

Hutt Kenny didn't want to stop, but he pulled in at Liberty, northeast of Houston, and filled the car up. Had the kid check everything, drove a couple blocks, saw a Dairy Queen, and stopped. Ordered steak fingers and fries, a vanilla coke malt. That was the thing about Dairy Queens, they'd make about anything you want. Grind up a candy bar, any kind you like, mix it right in or pour it on the top.

There were only four people inside, three girls in cheer-leader suits, two of them cute, the other maybe not. An old man sitting by himself. The old man was reading a paper, holding it high so he could check out some teenage leg. Kenny knew what he was doing, he'd done it a couple times himself.

The food was real good. Kenny got extra fries to go. Outside, the heat hit him hard. You're under the AC, it's worse when you get out again.

The phone booth was right by the door. They couldn't put the sucker *in*side, right?

Hutt didn't want to make the call, didn't want to talk to Junior now, later, any time at all. He dropped some coins in, listened for the tone. Nothing. Looked at the thing in his hand, saw it didn't have a cord.

"Fuck you," Hutt said, pissed off a little, mostly re-lieved that he couldn't make the call. Pissed off again be-cause Ma Bell had swallowed all his quarters, wouldn't give them back.

The Buick was baking, heat waves rising off the roof. He opened the door to let the hot air out. Leaned in and opened the far side too. And when he looked up, he saw the trooper in his brown uniform, in his cowboy boots, in his Smokey Bear hat.

"Shit," Kenny said, and knew, at once, the trooper had parked out back, and walked around the side. Which didn't mean a thing, cops were always doing that, looking for a freebie, talking up the high school girls. This one, though, wasn't doing either one. This one walked right up and said, "Afternoon, how we doin', sir?"

"Fine," Kenny said, "how are you?"

"Shoot, I could do without this heat."

"Me too," Hutt said, and wondered, his mind working down a little list, wondered if he had anything in the car, any shit that shouldn't be there, anything a cop would like to see. Decided he was fine, there was nothing there but an empty Coke can from the trip coming up.

"I like the Dairy Queen better'n any place in town," the cop said. "The food's good, they keep the place clean."

"I see one, I'm going to stop there," Hutt said. "I won't stop some place I don't know, something says **EATS** or **BARBECUE,** you don't know what you'll get there."

"That's the truth," the cop said.

"I like to be careful what I eat."

"Yes sir, more people ought.to do that."

"Some of these places, you see on the road, they oughta close them down."

"That's why a Dairy Queen always has plenty of customers. People know what they're going to get."

"They do. That's why they keep coming here."

"This your vehicle, sir?"

"What?"

"I said, this your vehicle, this your car, sir?"

"Yeah. Well, it's a rental, not mine."

The question, coming out of nowhere, rattled him some, took him by surprise. Up to then, they were doing okay, why did the guy start acting like a cop, everything's going just fine?

"Louisiana plates. That where you're from?"

"New Orleans," Hutt said.

The cop grinned. The grin said, I know what kind of stuff you clowns get away with down there. The cop took his hat off, took out a handkerchief and wiped the sweat off his face, down in his neck, up on his brow. His brow was half red, half fish-belly white from the Smokey Bear hat. He was forty, maybe, thinning hair and an ordinary face. Stripes on his sleeve, a plastic tag that read **KREET.** What the hell kind of name is that? Hutt thought. Probably some goddamn name like Cecil R. Dupree.

"Avis," said the cop, walking around the side, kicking at the tires. "You like the Park Avenue?"

"GM makes a good car," Hutt said.

"I'd rather have that than a Ford. We get Fords sometimes, then they'll do Chevy's a while. Can I see your license and insurance, sir?"

Hutt kept his cool, got his wallet out without shaking at all. Reached in the glove compartment, got the insurance paper out. The cop looked them over, looked up at Hutt.

"Mr. Hutt Kenny? This your current address?"

"Yes it is."

"I don't think I know anyone named Hutt."

I don't know any assholes named Kreet, Hutt thought.

"What you do down there, sir? You don't mind I ask?"

Hutt did. "Sales. Wholesale beverages and food."

"Uh-huh."

The cop gave Hutt a nod, walked around the side of the Dairy Queen and disappeared. Came back a minute later with his car. Stepped out and brought a sheet of paper up to Hutt.

"I just stopped you because you were out-of-state, sir. That's just routine, you didn't have any offense."

"I didn't think I did."

90

"The only thing is, I ran your name through, and a lot of bad shit come out. I don't guess you're surprised to hear that."

Hutt didn't answer. The cop glanced at his paper, back up to Hutt. "I got thirty-two arrests here, sir. Assault, assault, breaking and entering, possession of controlled substance, assault, assault, possession again, assault, assault—You assault folks a lot, Mr. Hutt."

"Kenny. It's Hutt Kenny, not Kenny Hutt."

"Yes, sir."

"That stuff you were reading. That's not right, that's a mistake."

"Which one is that, sir? There's thirty-two here."

"All of 'em. I was falsely charged, officer. If you got the record there, you know I was acquitted on every fucking one."

"I'd prefer you hold back on the obscenities, sir."

"Yeah, fine. Only what happened is, there's people in the same business I'm in, I'm just trying to make a living, okay? These people I'm talkin' about, every time I fuc— every time I turn around, they're accusing me of something I didn't even do. I never did any of that stuff you're reading there."

"Mr Kenny...." The cop folded up his paper and stuffed it in his pocket. "I've got no reason to hold you here. There's nothing I can charge you with, nothing you're wanted for. You want to get in your car and go, that's fine with me."

"Well...yeah, okay." Hutt felt a great sense of relief. The cop could see it too. Hutt didn't like that, but he didn't let it show.

"You're just doing your job," Hutt said, "what you're supposed to do."

"Have a good trip," the cop said.

Hutt got in his car. Put his seatbelt on, which he hardly ever did. The cop put his hands on the sill, leaned his head in. Looked at Kenny a second, looked kind of funny for a while, said, "Would you hit that trunk release for me, Mr. Kenny, then step outside of the car?"

"Huh? What for?"

""Cause I asked you to, sir."

"I don't get it. You said we were fine, you said it was all okay."

"Hit the release, and step out of the car, please, sir."

Hutt did. Something was wrong now, he didn't know what. The cop waited for him, waited so he'd be behind, and Hutt was in front. Walked him to the back, walked him to the big Buick trunk open wide.

Hutt took one quick look, made an awful sound, staggered back and covered up his eyes. The smell hit hard, hit him like a wall, hit him so hard he nearly fell. He could feel the steak fingers and the fries, The vanilla coke malt, everything he'd had for a year, was coming up fast. He swallowed hard, took a deep breath, held it all back.

"I didn't smell 'em till I leaned in the car, Mr. Kenny. Just a whiff is all. Figured something bad was back here. You acquainted with either of these persons, sir? You know who these fellas are?"

Hutt Kenny didn't, didn't know the joker with his zipper open and his pecker hanging out. Didn't know the guy in the aviator jacket that was black or maybe brown. Didn't know either one, but knew how they got there, knew who'd stuffed them in his trunk, and even knew why, fucking Cecil R. Dupree...

"I don't know 'em," Hutt said, "never saw them before in my life."

The cop shook his head. "I don't think I could stop at a Dairy Queen, something like that in the car. I sure couldn't handle that." He let his hand rest on the big black pistol at his side. "Might be good if you put your hands on your head now, sir. I expect you know how to do that..."

SIXTEEN...

Jack thought about Utah, Arizona, maybe Montana, somewhere he'd never been before, somewhere they'd never heard of Mexican Wells or Cecil Dupree. Canada maybe. Canada sounded fine. He'd seen a thing on the Travel Channel, it sounded okay. They had some nice babes up there, he'd seen them on the tube. French babes, too, and everybody knew what they liked to do.

What he couldn't do, he couldn't stay at Piggs. You kick Cat Eye in the nuts, you don't want to work on the same fucking planet anymore, you got to go somewhere else. Cecil wouldn't let Cat kill him, 'cause help is hard to find, but Jack knew he'd wish he was dead by the time Cat was through. Cat was good at that. Cat couldn't blink unless someone showed him how, but he knew how to hurt, he could hurt real good.

◆ ◆ ◆

The sun was blazing hot overhead by the time he slipped into the hole behind Wan's. He was tired, he was

93

beat, his gut was on fire, but he felt okay, he was feeling just fine. The cellar was cool, it was dark, and nobody knew he was there. Funny how the place could do that, make him feel safe, make him feel everything would turn out right. It fucking wouldn't, not until he got to the fucking North Pole or somewhere, but now it seemed fine.

When his gut cooled off, he wished he'd thought to slip into Wan's, make a butter and jelly, get something to drink. That's one thing he meant to do. Get a loaf of white bread, couple cans of something, bottles of water to keep down there.

"This is what I got to start doing," he said to himself, "I got to start thinking, got to start planning shit instead of just letting shit happen, which is what it's going to do you're not thinking ahead. You're not thinking, shit's thinking for you, and that's the kind of stuff you're going to get."

Jack lay back on the concrete floor and looked up in the dark. He could see little slits of light between the boards, but no one was up yet at Piggs, no one was moving about.

Funny how he wasn't even scared. He'd be scared later, when he had to figure some way to get a few bucks and get out of town, clear out of Texas before Cat knocked a few teeth out, broke a couple ribs. Canada was further off than Kansas. Further than the big square states that were stacked on top of that. A few bucks wouldn't cut it, he'd have to get his hands on a bundle for a jump like that.

See, there you go again, not planning or thinking, just letting shit flow through your head...

What did he think he was doing, running off to do dirty stuff with French babes, leaving Gloria behind? He didn't want girls like that, he wanted *her.* Jesus, what would she think, he did a thing like that? It'd break her fucking

94

heart, and they hadn't even had a date yet, hadn't even gone for pie.

Jack felt awful, and promised he'd make it up to her somehow. If he had to, he'd hold up a 7-Eleven, which would be a fucking chore. The way they did now, dumping cash right in the safe soon as some fucker gave them a twenty dollar bill, he might have to do three or four. If he had to, he would. He wondered if Ortega would let him borrow his car. He'd have to say it was medical, something like that. Jack didn't like to lie to friends, but he didn't know Ortega that well, and who else would let him have a car?

◆　◆　◆

Jack dreams about Cecil and Grape. They're talking, and Jack can hear everything they say. It's like he's a fly or something, sitting on the wall. He doesn't have to listen real hard, so maybe flies can hear better than we know.

"...So the fucking kid's calling, Junior himself, he's getting on the phone. I'm thinking, this little shit's not smart enough to dial, find the numbers on the phone."

"Junior, the old man's kid, he's calling, he's calling on the phone."

"What the fuck I tell you, Grape? I say the kid, he's calling on the phone. He's all upset, he's whining, you know, he's whining like a kid."

"Fucking little kid."

"That's what I'm saying. Fucking little kid. He's telling me the cops got Kenny Hutt. Kenny's in serious shit, they got him in Liberty County, they got him in the lockup there, they're finding some stiffs in his trunk, the guys are in a fucking rental car. This is all my fault, the kid's saying, I gotta do something, I got to get him out."

"Hutt Kenny, that's who we're talking 'bout here."

"What did I say?"

"Nothing, it's Hutt Kenny is all, it's not Kenny Hutt."

"I give a fuck? I give a fuck, some asshole from Maine or Vermont, he's got a Kenny and a Hutt?"

"This has got to do with Cat. I'm thinking it's got to do with Cat."

"It's got to do with Cat. Why am I telling you this, you know what it's all about? I'm putting this kid on hold, I'm looking for Cat, Cat's jackin' off somewhere. I'm saying, 'Cat, who's the other dude in the trunk, what the fuck's he doing in there?' 'Guy was pissin' onna wall,' Cat says, 'he shouldn't oughta do that.'"

"I hear him say that, I think I'm going to piss on myself. I'm trying not to laugh, I don't like to laugh, anything's got to do with Cat."

"You want to laugh, Grape, go ahead and laugh. Cat breaks your legs, I'm going to stand and watch."

"I told you, I'm not going to laugh. Not if it's got to do with Cat."

"I wouldn't, I was you."

"So you get back on the phone, you're talking to the kid."

"I get back on the phone, I'm telling the kid I don't know what he's talking about, I got nothing to do with what his guy's got in his trunk, and you shouldn't be telling me shit like this you're talking onna phone. I'm hanging up, he's calling back."

"I heard him calling back."

"He's saying, the phone's okay, I don't got to worry 'bout that. I'm saying, I'm glad to hear this, I'm worried anyway, I'm talking to a klutz like him. I tell him, fuck Kenny Hutt, fuck a guy wears a collar don't match his shirt. I'm saying, you want to sell your product, send me up a guy don't got any tassels on his shoes. Send me a guy, he's got a little respect."

"Hutt Kenny, that fuck, he don't know about respect."

"That's what I'm saying, that's what I'm telling fucking Ambrose Junior, Junior says wait a minute, I know he's talking to somebody else."

"He don't know what he's doing, he's talking to somebody else."

"That's what he's doing, it's not his old man, his old man's got troubles with his dick. He's coming back, then, he's saying, 'I'm sending a guy. He'll look okay, he won't be dressing like Hutt. But we still got to do a partial, Mr. Dupree, and don't take offense at that.'

"I tell him fuck the partial, you little prick. You want all the pay, you bring all the shit. Keep it, you don't want to do that."

"You're hanging up on the kid."

"I'm hanging up, the kid isn't calling back."

"He'll send a guy, he's not backing out."

"Fucking guy's in his car right now, Grape, you can bet on that. Junior's a prick, but he's his old man's kid. He ain't about to back up."

"Fucking guy's on his way. The kid wants the deal, he isn't backing out."

"What did I say? What did I fucking say just now? Get me somethin' to eat, I don't want nothing Chink, get me something else. And get that fucker Jack. You find him, I don't care where the fuck he is, I want him here, I want him *now,* you get that little shit back to Piggs..."

SEVENTEEN...

Ever'body they lookin' for you, mahn. Grape he coming here talking to me. Where the fock Jhack is? I am saying, how the fock I know, Grape he hitting me beside the head, you see? I getting hitted for you, Jhack. Don' be coming here, dey hitting me some more, I don' liking dat."

Jack didn't listen. He sat on the floor, hunched in the corner, scrooched in the corner in the kitchen at Wan's, squatted in the corner stuffing rice in his mouth, rice from last night or the night before that, shoveling that rice, gulping water from a glass, rice falling out of the corners of his mouth.

"Mahn, you making me sick, you know dhat?" Ahmed said, "I am raised in the focking desert, we got better manner than dat. What you do, man, pissing ever'body off, why these som'bitches lookin' for you?"

"Rhino coming in? I don't want to be here, he's coming in. Rhino going to go right to Cecil, tell him where I am."

"Me, *I* am going to Cecil, tell him where you are, you don' get outta here. Gimme the bowl, you got enough of thees crap. You going to be 'sploding like a boomb, you know dat? You know what is happen, dey throwin' rice at the weddings? The pigeons is eating the rice, dey drinkin' some'ting, dey 'sploding. Jus' like dat."

"That's rice hasn't been cooked, you fucking raghead. If it was, 'bout a million fuckin' chinks's be exploding every day."

"I am cooking Al Denny. You cooking dat way, you hardly cookin' at all."

"I never heard of nothin' like that."

"This is because you a fockin' waiter an a deeshwasher, Jhack. Fockin' waiter don' have to know 'bout Al Denny or nothin' else. Gotta carry plates an' shit, dat is all you got to know."

"I kicked Cat in the balls. Last night at Piggs. I didn't mean to but I did."

"Shit, man…" Ahmed slammed his hands against his head, slammed his head twice. Rolled his eyes, did his Arab act, said "faya-baba-daba," or words to that effect.

"This is a bad t'ing to do, I t'ink he goin' to kill you for dat. This is what they doing in my country, mahn, only there they doin' it twice."

Jack was beginning to think Ahmed was right. All that rice, he was swelling up fast. Not to the point of explosion, but close enough to throw up, or something worse than that.

"You ever been to Canada? I'm thinking another country's the way to go now."

"I am t'ink you maybe right," Ahmed said. He washed Jack's bowl and put it on a stack. Anybody wants to look, nobody's used a bowl, all the bowls are in a stack.

"I t'ink I would go somewhere else. Is fockin' cold in Canada. I am t'inking Whatamala, mahn."

"What?"

"Whatamala. Is hot, mahn, you don' freeze you ass off, you got a beach down there."

"I don't think so. Everyone down there's a Mescan or something close. I wouldn't like it at all."

Ahmed laughed. When he laughed, Jack could see his bad teeth. He could understand that. You wouldn't have a lot of dentists, out in the desert like that. You're a dentist, you can do a lot better nearly anywhere else.

"What you don' like, Jhack, is people who maybe got a name like Ricky Chavez, somethin' like dat. Maybe someone got a bank or somet'ing, is liking someone you are liking too."

"Hey, just can that kind of talk, okay?" Jack pulls himself up off the floor, which isn't easy, his stomach is cramping up fast.

"I thought we was some kind of friends, Ahmed. I'm not talking 'bout friends that like each other, I'm talking the other kind that don't."

"I t'ink that's what we got."

"Yeah, well you don't show it much. I come here thinking I can maybe talk to somebody, all I'm getting is rice ain't even hardly cooked. That and shit 'bout Ricky Chavez and that other part I don't appreciate."

"Don' be getting you hair up in the air, Jhack. You maybe t'inkin, Ahmed, who is not my friend, he is tellin' Cecil, he is tellin' Cat, Jhack is livin' in the doggie place, he is livin' under Piggs. You t'ink I tellin' them dat? You hurting *my* feelings, Jhack, an' I don' 'preciate that."

"What? I ain't living in no dog place, what you talking about?"

"Hey, I see you comin' out the hole, like the rhabeet or somet'in, Jhack. I know there is the Gino's Fine Fish Restaurante before the Piggs, and the Sunset Vet before dat. I know these t'ing because I am cook for the Gino's and putting the puppy dog to sleeping at the vet. I am feel so very sad, I am doing that.

"Don' be tellin' me what's where an' what's not. De places is changing, but Ahmed is not. I am being here all the time, Jhack."

"Jesus," Jack said. He wished his belly didn't hurt so bad, he'd whack the fucking Arab right there, see if Ortega would loan him the car, take off right now. Fuck Ortega if he didn't like it, he'd whack the Swede greaser too. And while he's thinking, Ahmed's thinking too, and he's gone, vanished, out the kitchen door, leaving Jack no better off than he was before...

EIGHTEEN...

$\mathbf{G}$loria Mundi sits in the pilot's seat of the Junkers JU-52. She rests her hands easy on the wheel, which is just like the wheel of a Ford or a Buick or any other car, except the upper part's gone It isn't broken, it's simply not there. Beside her, to her right, is another seat, with another wheel, just like the one in front of her. This is where the copilot sat. Gloria is certain the steering wheel's made like this to help the pilots see. She's taller than the average girl, and it's still hard to see out the front or out the sides. It's cramped in there, and everything's small.

It was surely cramped for Hauptmann Wilhelm Klass, who was six-feet-three, and a good hundred-eighty-two pounds. All this Gloria figured from the way Germans measure things, which is not the same as ours. Gloria looked it up in the library over to Luling one day. The lady there gave her a look, and said she remembered the war, and wondered why an American would want to know stuff like that.

Gloria didn't mind, she was plenty used to that. Her daddy hadn't built the **BATTLE OF BRITUN FAMILY**

FUN PARK to show off German skills in the air. He'd built it to show those Kraut motherfuckers they'd lost. Daddy had other colorful descriptions but that was his favorite of all.

Daddy hadn't fought in the war, he'd barely been born at the time. But he had a good background from comic books and movies with Audie Murphy and Alan Ladd. He'd watched "Hogan's Heroes" and knew what he liked, and what he didn't like at all.

Considering the times, Gloria felt that was likely fair. That's where Daddy was coming from, and the library lady as well. Germans weren't our friends at the time. Especially fucking Nazi butchers with acne and piggy little eyes who struck without warning from the air. That was the worst kind of all. If you went through the **BATTLE OF BRITUN** at the time, you could see these butchers, plaster pilots formerly from Fricker's Mens Store, dying in the cockpits of Heinkels, Arados, and Messerschmitts of every shape and size. They were splashed with red paint, and had real bullet holes from Daddy's .45. When the park closed down for the night, Daddy liked to roam about with a bottle of Vat 69, and shoot Germans in the head. For a while, there was screaming from the bad PA, but tourists didn't seem to like that.

Still, Gloria couldn't bring herself to hate Hauptmann Wilhelm Klass for what he might have done at the time. Could never bring herself to feel that way, for he was the only man she'd ever loved at all. Fate and the cruel years had deemed they'd never meet in this life, but that didn't mean they'd always be apart. Gloria believed this was true. She felt she knew Wilhelm better than she knew a lot of people living at the time.

Whatever he'd done so bad, he'd done it some sixty years past, and so had a lot of folks as well. Shoot, was he any worse than Cat Eye or Grape or Cecil R. Dupree? Lord

God, he'd have to be pretty fucking bad to get as low as that.

Gloria could look at the faded picture on Wilhelm's ID, stuck right there on the panel with all the little dials since 1943, and look in his faded blue eyes and *know* he was good inside. One thing for sure—you're dancing buck naked every night for a bunch of truckers and such, you sure as hell know about eyes. You know what some fella's thinking, and it isn't always what you'd imagine it would be. Sometimes, it's something you wouldn't ever guess. And the thing she saw in Wilhelm's eyes went right to her heart, touched something there that always brought the hot tears, made her know he was with her somehow, right there close by.

"We're going to make it," she said, "I just know it's so." The words caught in her throat like they always did, and she gripped the wheel tight right where his hands had been.

"We're going to make it, and you're going to fly again, Will. And you don't have to be a Kraut motherfucker this time, either, you can be whatever you like. Whatever it is, hon, my love for you isn't never going to change..."

NINETEEN...

"Where I find him, you know where the little fuck is, you know where he is? He's in the fucking back, got his head in the dumpster back of Wan's, he's tossing up, for Christ sake. That's what he's doing, little fuck is throwing up."

"You told me what he's doing, don't tell me what he's doing no more, I don't want to hear the little fuck is throwing up."

Cecil turned to Jack. "Why you doing that, Jack? You eat somethin' bad, why you throwing up?"

"I guess I eat something bad," Jack said. "All I can figure is I eat something bad, Mr. Dupree."

Grape laughed. "He might've eat something bad."

"Shut up, Grape. I got fuckin' ears as good as you."

Cecil looked at Jack like he always did, like he was looking at a bug, at a wall, at a real exciting brick somewhere. Jack looked at Cecil like he always did, like he wasn't looking anywhere at all. That was the best way to look at Cecil R. Dupree. You look at Cecil, look at his fat little fingers, look at his toes, look at him anywhere at all,

Cecil figures you're looking at his face, you're looking at his strawberry mask, you're thinking "Hi, Ho, fucker!" and Cecil's going to get you for that.

"Cat thinks he oughta cut off your balls, something on that order, Jack. I told him, I told him Jack didn't strike you with harmful intent, he's not as dumb as that, he wouldn't do somethin' like that. Cat don't think that's right, he ought to get you back, but you know Cat, he don't know how to stop.

"I don't need no cripple, some fuck washin' dishes with a stump, I got no use for that. So you get out of this, Jack, you don't get hurt or nothing, all right? I already tol' Cat you're sorry, you don't gotta do that. Best thing to do don't get in his way for a while, don't do nothing, you unnerstan' that?"

"I surely do, and I appreciate what you done, Mr. Dupree," Jack said, careful not to look anywhere at all. "That was a kindly thing to do, I sincerely mean that."

"He says it's a kindly thing to do," Grape said. "The fuck's saying that. You gotta say, 'you're welcome, Jack, wasn't nothing at all.'"

"You want to watch that mouth," Cecil said. "I need someone show me how to talk, I'll get me fucking Tom Rather, some New York fuck's got better talk than you."

"That was a joke, Cecil. Wasn't nothing more than that."

"I want a joke, Grape, I'll get me fucking Dave Leno, some dude like that. Go get me some ribs over to Lockhart, don't get no sausage or nothing, get me some ribs and don't eat one on the way. You eat my ribs I'll smell it on your breath. Don't eat a fucking mint. You do, I'll smell that too, I'll know what you're covering for, we clear on that?"

"Yes, sir, Cecil, we sure are clear on that."

"It's Mr. Dupree till I'm not pissed anymore, you figure when that'll be. Jack, what you doin' standing 'round here? I have saved your life, what more you want out of me? God damn, I got you and Grape an' Cat, I got me the whole Three Stooges, now what in the fuck did I do to deserve a crew like that?"

◆ ◆ ◆

"He said, what he said was he isn't going to let Cat get back at me at all. Said I was out of that, 'cause I didn't do anything with harmful intent. That means it wasn't on purpose, so I don't have to get hurt or maimed or nothing like that."

"I know about this harmful intent," Ortega said. "This is something you can do hard time for, you messin' with the law."

"Is batter you got the law on you back, you got the Caht," Ahmed said. "Sometime they don' kill you too much, you dealin' wit' the law."

"This is true here. It's not so true, I'm sorry to say, you're down in Mexico. We still have some problems there, which will be solved shortly by our new president."

"Hey, you don' wan' to get toss in the greaser jail, thas bad t'ing to do."

"You watch that Middle Eastern mouth of yours, *amigo*. You don't want to be doing no ethnic slurring with me."

"I don' have the harmful intent, so ees okay. You can't do not'in to me."

Ahmed was seized by his sudden flash of humor, seized to such degree he was forced to clutch his stomach to hold the joy in.

Jack doesn't laugh. Jack dumps dishes in a warm and soapy sea, in a sea afloat with pork, shrimp, chicken, bits and pieces of creatures of every sort, in a psuedo-chink whatever sort of sea, whatever Ahmed imagines at the time.

The food at Wan's has little to do with the menu at all, for the people who stop here don't know shit from Szechwan. What they know is Piggs is next door, they can chase down the food with a Shiner or a Bud, step across the way, gaze at something hot as chili pepper, sweet as ginger rice, something they wouldn't dare order up at home.

"Once I am driving trock to Qal'a Sharqat, I am seein' dis guy he is havin' flaht, he is havin' two flaht what he is havin', one on de fron' one on de bahk. Is hunert twenny somet'ing, which is not so bahd in Qal'a Sharqat, this is the cool time of de year, you know?"

"Yeah, when's that?"

"When is the what?"

"When's the fucking cool time of the year?"

"Why you askin dat?" Ahmed is annoyed when he's talking and someone else is talking too.

"Why you askin dat, you never hear of thees place, you don' know where is Qal'a Sharqat, you wanna know when is cool up dere. Is south of Mosul and Al Qaiyara. Is north of Tkrit. You t'ink you got it now?"

"*Bueno,* I got it now."

"You don' got *sheet,* mahn—"

Ahmed raised his big steel cleaver and came down with a *whack,* with a shudder, with a fervor and a glee that plastered green onions to the ceiling and the wall. One green snip hit Ortega right between the eyes. Jack was near certain the Ay-rab could see Mescan fingers go *shick-shick-shick* beneath his blade, see the sever, see the hack, see the slick little stubbies bounce about.

He knew this was so, knew it was going on right in Ahmed's head. Knew everyone who worked in the place thought Ahmed was a clown, eighty-two pounds of camel shit, but Jack knew better than that.

It made him itch in the middle of his back to know Ahmed was aware of his hidey-hole under Piggs, that it wasn't a secret anymore, someone knew he was there. Ahmed might tell someone or maybe not. A person of the Arab persuasion could turn on you just like that, they did it all the time, everybody knew that.

Ortega was humming some Mescan tune, thinking, maybe, how whales were doing something evil, grinning down there in the deep because no one knew their true nature at all, no one but Ortega who knew they were Satan's minions of the sea.

The more he thought about it, the more he felt bad about using Ortega's car to run away, and he was glad he'd decided to stay. Not *stay*, but not exactly go, not until he hit a couple stores so he could take Gloria Mundi out for pie, ask her to quit and go away. Tell her he had enough money, she wouldn't have to do what she was doing anymore.

Sure, she'd told him she *liked* what she was doing, but a stripper, what's she going to say? Man, I really love stomping naked under red and purple lights, wearing these godamn shoes, showing all my parts to a bunch of assholes, it's a fun thing to do.

Course she didn't like it. There wasn't a nice girl would. Okay, maybe Maggie and Alabama Straight and Whoopie LaCrane, but Gloria wasn't like that. What Gloria needed was a guy who could see how fine and decent she was with all her clothes on, you can't see her tits or nothing else. And you can't get that from some fucking Mex got gold on his boots and candy you can get at the Walgreen's store...

"You got nothing to do, I will find you something, you fuck. Mr. Cecil Dupree isn't paying you to stand 'round watchin' a Ay-rab cook."

111

NEAL BARRETT, JR.

Jack did a little jump, did a little hop before he could stop, and cussed himself for letting Rhino come up behind him like that.

"I was just getting to these dishes, finish 'em up," Jack said. "There isn't but a few, I'll be done with 'em quick."

"Don't let me stand in your way, then. I wouldn't fool with a man's work ethic, Jack. You just dive right fuckin' in."

Jack didn't move because Rhino's eyes were an inch or two from his, which said Jack better not move till Rhino was through. That was a hard thing to do, because Rhino had little B.B. eyes hidden under rolls of baby fat. Little black eyes, cookie dough fat, and pores the size of craters with stuff coming out. Rhino looked like Yellowstone Park, everything bubbling and oozing all the time.

Even worse was the way Rhino smelled. Everyone thought he got the name from his size, but it wasn't that at all. He smelled like a rhino. Not like a human or anything else. No one in town had ever smelled a rhino, but no one had to, everyone knew.

"I fear I been hearing reports on your behavior, Jack," Rhino said. Rhino knew exactly how long Jack could hold his breath, and grinned when he had to let it out. "You in a little trouble, seems to me."

"I made a mistake, is all," Jack said. "I talked about it to Mr. Dupree. He said it wasn't no harmful intent."

"I heard that too. An' I don't give a fuck about your intent, boy. This is not the kind of employee de-portment I am happy with, you unnerstan' that?"

"I surely do. I understand that."

Jack didn't have to turn and look. He knew Ortega and Ahmed had managed to disappear. Jack didn't blame them for that. Rhino's slinging shit, you don't want any to land on you.

112

PıGGS

"You want to keep straight, you want to be happy in your work, you want to get along with me?"

"Yes, sir, I guess that's what I want to do."

"You guess? What is fucking guess, Jack? *Guess* ain't a *word* you be *usin'* on *me...*"

And Rhino pokes and punches each word right into Jack's chest, pokes with a finger hard as a sap, pounds it and grinds it, jabs it to the bone, and Jack, clearly not thinking, not thinking at all, pushes this fat, intrusive finger aside, not like he's mad, not so Rhino can take the gesture wrong, maybe kill him on the spot, maybe stomp him flat.

"Hell, I never done anything to piss you off," Jack said, not backing off at all, "you got no cause to be stompin' on me. You talk like I'm fuckin' off alla time and that ain't so. I do what you tellin' me, takin' your shit, whatever you dishing out. You got no right jumping on me, I'm not doing nothing worse than nobody else."

Rhino simply looked at Jack, gazed at him with his cold and scary eyes, eyes that were tiny ball bearings in a 40-weight pit. For an instant, for a second and a half, Jack was fairly certain he didn't have a chance, that Rhino would do him right there.

Then, he saw something in those eyes he couldn't make out. Something uncertain, something like doubt. Something like pieces of a puzzle Rhino couldn't figure out.

Then, in a blink, he was Rhino again, breath like a dead man, pores full of shit.

"Get to those dishes, get 'em done quick," he told Jack. "And don't be talkin' uncivil to me, don't be doing that again."

It was over, and Jack was still alive, and Rhino was gone...

113

TWENTY...

Jack figured you could walk into Piggs any time of the year. You'd been in a coma, say, didn't know it was Christmas or Easter or the Fourth of July. Nothing had changed, nothing was different from the time you'd been before.

Once, he couldn't say when, taking a pee or eating a Mars, he was struck with wisdom unaware, and saw why people came into Piggs, why they did it all the time. They didn't want a fucking tree, they didn't want a purple egg. What they wanted was to get away from people who did. Family and friends and uncles and aunts. Wives, who wanted to fucking *drive* somewhere with the kids in the back and a battleship dragging ass behind.

They didn't want something different, they wanted things the same. They wanted girls to take their clothes off as nature had intended them to do. They wanted to have a cold beer, and they didn't want to go home ever again.

And Jack, squeezing through the raucous, happy, semiconscious crowd, juggling a tray of Five-Spice Chicken, Moo Shu Pork, Hunan Beef and Kung Po Shrimp above

115

his head, knew he was afflicted as well, that he had the fever too, that it might be Tuesday or Friday afternoon. It might be Sunday, for Piggs was open on the Lord's day as well. The gang in Piggs was grateful for pussy, and didn't think God would take offense at all.

Jack forgot who had ordered what, and no one complained, for it tasted all the same. Four lawyers and a judge, all from San Antone, and the only law they knew was Maggie Thatch, riding on the judge's chubby knee.

"You seen Gloria or what," Jack asked her. "She's supposed to be on, she isn't anywhere."

"Shit, Jack, I am busy here, all right? How'd I know?"

"I thought you might is all."

"Well I don't, and you are interfering with my customer's delight."

"I can't see how I'm doing that."

A lawyer with a beard tried to see around Jack. "I can't see the ladies, you standing there, son. Get us a couple Buds all around."

"I'm your food person," Jack said, "you got to see a wait person 'bout that."

The lawyer said "fucking little fag," or words to that effect. Jack left a bill for $38.97, making up tax in his head, adding five bucks, certain these assholes wouldn't leave a tip.

◆ ◆ ◆

He brought a plate of buffalo wings to a customer at the bar. Stopped, on the way back to Wan's, saw Gloria just as she vanished through the dressing room door, turned and followed her in.

"I'm on, Jack, I can't stop and talk right now."

Gloria didn't bother to turn around. She stood at the mirror, doing that thing girls do when they're putting their lipstick on, like they're coming up for air, breathing like a fish.

"And don't come bargin' in like that. Maggie and Alabama don't like it, they're going to get a lock."

"I'm a authorized employee, Gloria. And don't be putting any locks on here, that's a fire code violation's what it is. I'll catch hell for that."

"Well don't be doing it then. Don't be barging in."

Gloria dropped her robe, let it fall around her feet, and Jack felt his heart try to jump out of his chest. He could see her naked a hundred times a day, didn't matter how many, it was always the same.

Sometimes she looked like a statue, the ones in magazines. Perfect all over, not a zit or a mole. That was easy, you were marble, some kind of stone, but a real girl, that was something else again.

"You going to stand there an' look all day? My God, Jack, I feel like I ought to put clothes on you come around. It isn't a natural thing, looking like that."

"I want you and me to go out. We talked about it, you said you liked Denny's just fine, you wouldn't mind a pie. You said you liked it cold and I said so did I."

"I know we talked about that. There just hasn't been time."

"I know about the *time,* all right. You got plenty to do, I guess I'm aware of that."

Gloria turned to face him, no blemish, no blotch, no mark of any kind. No anger, no flush, not anything at all, and he wished she liked him more than that.

"You got somethin' on your mind, Jack, it better not be 'bout private personal business of mine. If it is, you surely better keep it to yourself 'cause I will not put up with intrusions on my life. I have spent a great deal of time working up the strength to assert my inner self. That is *mine,* and you will not fuck with it, friend, not you or anyone else."

"I'm just saying, you take it any way you like, but I mean it as a friend. Any pretense at true romance from Ricky Chavez is as cheap as that candy he's carryin' around. An' I'd think twice you let him in your home. Don't matter how rich a greaser gets, he sees something lyin' around, it's gone, okay? No racial offense, that's just the way it is. I hope you'll think about that."

Gloria looked away, looked at anything but Jack.

"I can only imagine you are real uncertain of yourself right now. I'm sure it has to do with that awful incident with Cat, and your anger is spilling on me. That's the way I'll try to see it in my head. If I can find the will for that, I might be able to speak to you again. You will know if that happens. If it doesn't, stay out of my way, and I am talking fucking forever, you hear me, Jack?"

"It's that Mescan thing, isn't it? I hadn't said that, we'd be all right."

"No, we wouldn't be *all right*. You got some real abrasive qualities, Jack, things you're gonna have to hone down. Jesus, I don't know if you even understand that."

"Yeah, I do. It's been mentioned to me before."

"Then you got somewhere to start."

Jack looked at her. "I was going to pull a couple jobs, get some ahead. I thought I had something to offer, you'd see me in a different light, see me different than I am. First I was going to take Ortega's car. Now I kinda see that's a ignoble thing to do."

"My God, you sound like someone deranged, you know what? You scare the hell out of me, you talk like that."

"No, what you're hearing's not that. I think what you said, Gloria, what you said tonight, that's already working inside. I think what it is, I've grown a little tonight..."

"You what?"

"What I said, you know? You hit on stuff I need to work on in myself, and I appreciate that. One thing is, I have not thought about Mescans as much as I should. I'm going to think more about 'em now."

"I'd stay off of that if I was you."

"Huh-uh, that's what I been doing, Gloria. I been letting racial shit stand in the way of my personal regards. I don't *like* fucking Mescans, okay? But that's not the thing, I don't like Ortega and he's a friend. I don't like him in a *different* way I don't like Ricky Chavez. I didn't see that clear till I was talking 'bout him to you."

"Didn't see what, Jack?"

"Ricky Chavez is one rich greaser. Ortega's poor as a dog. You wouldn't think about doing it with someone like him."

"Doing it."

"You know. Doing it."

"Yeah, I do know, you stupid son of a bitch." Gloria's eyes turned so cold, Jack thought he might come down with the flu right there.

"Sometimes words don't come out the way I want 'em to," he said, certain this would take him nowhere at all. "That's a shortcoming I hope to work on as well."

"Don't *work* on nothing for me, all right? Don't trouble yourself, don't hurt your fucking head."

Gloria turned away abruptly and snatched the robe off her chair, slipped it on and held it tight around the neck.

"Now what's that for?" Jack looked pained. "What'd I do?"

"I am not comfortable talking to you naked anymore, Jack, and I feel bad about that. I feel you have broken a bond between us."

"What kinda bond was that? You won't even go out for pie."

119

"Maybe pie just wasn't meant to be, hon." She checked her hair in the mirror, licked her little finger, and brushed a curl across her cheek.

"If it wasn't, you know, it's a whole lot easier to find out now. Sometimes it's best you nip something like that before it gets to pie..."

TWENTY-ONE...

Cecil was making a big thing out of a guy in a black Stetson hat, some singer Jack had seen on TV. The guy had a short girl with him, and she was a singer too, maybe twelve, thirteen, but made up older than that. They both wore cowboy suits with flowers and cactus sewn on the shirts, and the same kind of boots. The girl had hardly any tits, and thick legs she covered with a fringe.

The singers were autographing pigs. The girl singer picked one up and the little pig squealed and the little girl laughed and kissed it on the head. The pig was one of three new piglets romping about in the big glass tanks, in place of the three that had gotten too big, and Rhino had taken next door the night before. The pigs would go to Tex Savallo, the butcher, and come back as barbecue sandwiches Cecil sold for three ninety-five at the bar.

This was a truth Jack had stumbled on some time before. A sandwich is a sandwich and a pig is a pig. That was a fact any kid over four could plainly see, but no one connected the two. People thought about cows and they thought about steaks. But they didn't think about them at the very same time. What people did, they filed things away in their heads where they wanted them to be. Like *fuck* is over here, and your dick falling off from some awful disease is over there. Jack wondered if Ahmed and Ortega knew about this, and decided he'd tell them sometime.

❖ ❖ ❖

Jack was always glad to see celebrities in the place. They kept Cecil occupied, and Cecil kept Grape and Cat busy playing hoods. Singers and movie people liked to hang around guys who'd whacked somebody, or knew someone who did.

Grape was the loudmouth skinny guy on *Sopranos,* and Cat was the dope. There was no one on the show like Cecil R. Dupree. There was no one like Cecil anywhere.

Jack took an order of Ahmed's recycled eggrolls to a table of college boys. They'd been there half the night, and were drunk enough to eat lint. Minnie Mouth was dancing naked, rubbing up one guy then the next. Jack was sure she was asleep. The college guys had stuffed so many bills in her shoes, she could hardly raise her knees.

When Gloria came on again, he stood in the dark where he could see real good, and no one like Cecil or Grape could see him. Every time he watched her it was always the same, a flutter in his belly, and a moment when he couldn't catch his breath.

Sometimes he'd imagine her dressed in fine clothes like they had in ladies' magazines. You weren't supposed to open magazines in a store, but a lot of times he did.

Once, when he borrowed Ortega's car, he found a *Victoria's Secret* catalog buried under the otter and whale magazines. The pictures knocked him for a loop. He wanted to order Gloria a hot little number but he didn't know her size, and knew better than to ask.

And that was the thing, he thought, he had good ideas, stuff he'd like to do, but when it came time, nothing seemed to work right. He'd fucked up good with that Mescan talk, she didn't like that. There wasn't going to be any pie if he didn't figure how to do it right.

❖ ❖ ❖

He was thinking on that, running some ideas by, when it struck him there wasn't any music going on, there wasn't any girls. What there was, was Cecil R. Dupree over at the DJ's, standing in the dark.

Now what is this shit? Jack wondered, backing away a little farther from the bar. He didn't like it, whatever the hell it might be. Stuff you don't know about, that's the stuff you don't like to see.

"We got a special surprise for y'all at Piggs tonight," Cecil said, holding the mike so close it squealed in everyone's ears.

"What we got is *post* time, ladies an' gents, if there's any ladies here," and everybody whoops at that, everybody knows there's not. "What I'm saying is you don't have to go to Kentucky or nothing, we got your race right here."

The guys cheered, whistled and stomped. They didn't know what was coming, didn't have any idea. Didn't care, as long as the girls got naked and Piggs didn't run out of beer.

"We got your horsies, we got 'em right here. Ugliest horsies I ever seen, but take a look at them jockeys, fellas, that's what you come here to see!"

Branford Marsalis blew out the chords of "Dewey Baby," which didn't sound Derby at all. Nobody heard, they were all on their feet, cheering as the red and purple

123

lasers raked across the floor, catching the horsies as they bolted out of the gate on all fours.

Jack stared at the sight, wondering who'd come up with this, wondered exactly why. It wasn't like Cecil to give away anything free. Everything cost something at Piggs. The only thing you could do without paying was pee, to make room for more beer.

Jack recognized some of the horsies. A lawyer who came in every night, the dude who sold cars. A trucker he hadn't seen before, a big dude Maggie said was a defrocked Steeler guard. They all had numbers pinned on their butts, and the naked jockeys—in little jockey hats—whipped their mounts freely as they scrambled across the floor.

Minnie Mouth and Laura Licks. Maggie Thatch and Alabama Straight. All the girls except Gloria Mundi. Gloria wasn't there.

Jack squinted through the dark, through the dizzy laser lights, looked until he found her, caught her in the crowd. Wished, in that moment, he was anywhere else. Kansas, Oklahoma, even Arkansas. Anywhere but Piggs in Mexican Wells, watching the woman he loved hanging on the greaser, hanging on Ricky Chavez.

Okay, not hanging on, but close enough to make Jack's stomach knot up, get the antifreeze leaking again. One hand on his shoulder, saying something to him, looking up at him, not even watching the race going on. Ricky looking *down,* looking in her robe, taking everything in, her not trying to close it up at all.

What was she saying, come on up, climb up to my place, you can do anything you like—Aw, man, she wasn't saying that, not to this taco with his banks and his fucking candy on sale from the Walgreen's store. Not Jack's Gloria, not the woman he'd be with forever, soon as he could straighten everything out...

A shout went up from the crowd, a din, a near explosion you could hear as far as Fort Worth. The trucker had gone down hard, spilling Maggie Thatch, sending her sprawling, ass over end, an aerial view of her private inner parts. Everyone had seen most of Maggie a dozen times before, but this was a special event, this didn't cost you anything at all.

Halfway to the finish line, the lawyer drew ahead, the used car dude and the Steeler dropped behind. Jack decided, at exactly that moment, that he had to kill Ricky Chavez. It came to him just like that. He felt a lot better with that off his mind. The only thing was where, he'd have to think about that. Not right at Piggs, that wouldn't be a smart thing to do. Somewhere else, somewhere far off. Which meant he'd have to borrow Ortega's car.

Would that be the right thing to do? Jack wondered. Was there a conflict here, if the owner of the car was of the greaser persuasion too?

It was something to consider, and Jack would have given it some thought, if someone hadn't wrapped a big hand across his mouth, yanked him off his feet and dragged him out the side door.

Jack knew at once who had him, and the knowledge struck terror in his heart. No one had more lethal body odor, no one had hands the size of Cat's.

Jack kicked, flailed at empty air, tried frantically to shake himself free. Nothing helped, nothing did any good at all. From the corner of his eye, he could see the dumpster back of Wan's, the twenty-watt bulb above the door. Maybe Ahmed or Rhino would walk out and see him. Maybe Cat wouldn't kill him in front of the help—

Cat held him high, held him out straight. Someone took off his shoes, peeled off his socks. Jack got a look, saw it was Grape, saw his bad teeth, saw his nasty smile. Looked right at him as Grape ripped his T-shirt off his

125

chest. Jack felt his jeans slide down his legs, felt his shorts go next.

Oh God, they're going to do it, they're going to cut it off, don't let 'em do that!

It was over, over and done. A minute, a minute and a half, and Jack had never been so frightened in his life. He was scared, he was naked, and somehow he wasn't outside anymore, he was back inside Piggs. Down on the floor, down on his knees. Down on his knees and something heavy, lumpy on his back. Looked to the left, looked to the right, saw a pair of hand-tooled boots, six-hundred retail in South Fort Worth, a grand in New York.

A fringe hung down and tickled his nose. Jack smelled girl sweat, leather, cigarettes and beer.

Grape leaned down real close, whispered in his ear: "Cecil said he wasn't gonna let Cat kill you, Cecil does what he says he's gonna do. This here's what *you* gotta do. Move, you little fuck."

Jack gasped as Grape kicked him soundly in the rear. Jack scrambled off as fast as he could across the floor. He could hear Cat laughing, a deep, terrible, totally mindless sound, a haw-haw-haw without pleasure, anger, anything at all.

The lasers seared his eyes, the mean little boots dug in his sides. His hands got dirty, his knees went numb. Butts, egg rolls, peanuts, and mud passed beneath his eyes. Once he saw a twenty dollar bill.

"Hold it, folks," shouted Cecil R. Dupree, chewing on the mike, "we got a late entry here, it ain't done yet!"

Clap, shout, stomp on the floor. We want more-more-more.

"Here she is, ladies an' gents, y'all know her, our real special guest an' she's just fourteen, the prettiest songbird in Nashville, Tennessee...little miss Kandy Klee!"

PIGGS

Jack wished he was dead, a wish he'd had once or twice before. God wouldn't listen to him then, wouldn't listen now.

"Thirteen, asshole," said little Kandy Klee, but only Jack could hear...

TWENTY-TWO

One of the things Ricky thought about airplanes was he didn't care for them at all. Didn't like getting in one, didn't like it when they got up off the ground. It didn't help any that Gloria's plane was wedged in forever in a live oak tree, and hadn't taken off since 1943.

True, it was stationary now, but it was the nature of things that went up to come down. Even the birds, which the Creator had intended to fly, sometimes dropped for no reason at all.

Nevertheless, if the *gringo* devil himself could climb up here, so could Ricardo Garcia Chavez, for he was assuredly twice the man the Godless gangster Cecil would ever be.

And, besides, he would hang by his *cojones* from a fucking balloon if he could win the heart of Gloria Mundi, and call her his own.

"One cannot but admire the genius of the German people," Ricky said. "Yes, it is true they have often turned their talent to the art of the wars, but they can craft the most incredible machines.

"This thing of the air is a marvel to see, Miss Mundi. I, Ricky Chavez, have never been in such a device before, and I am grateful you have allow me to experience the Junkers JU 52, which I recall has a maximum speed of 350 kilometers an hour, and the ceiling of 18,045 feet, yes?"

"That's true," Gloria said, "though that's goin' to depend on your load, an' what kind of weather you might be up against in the European skies. You got your performance numbers, see, and you got your ever'day variable type conditions, which isn't going to always be the same."

"That is much like life itself, is it not, Miss Mundi?" Ricky sighed as he peered into the night through the open portside door, standing well back in case his stomach rebelled, which was likely at such a distance to the ground.

"What we expect of the goals to which we strive is not always that which the person achieves. Sometime, we are falling short of this."

"I guess," Gloria said. "I hadn't given it a whole lot of thought."

She had, as a fact, but wasn't about to get into something deep as that. Deep, with a guy, led to the very same thing that shallow did, but it took them more time to get where they were going, which was right in your crotch, where Ricky Chavez was gazing now.

Chavez was all right, but he thought he was slick as Johnson's Wax. A man just couldn't be easy with a woman, he couldn't stop thinking what he was doing there. Every time a man opened his mouth, he told you a little more he didn't want you to know.

Lord, he'd gone and looked up that speed and ceiling stuff on the net or in a book, and thought she couldn't figure that out. He didn't know shit about German aircraft, anyone could see that.

And, she reminded herself, she hadn't "allowed" him to experience being there, hadn't asked him up at all. Any

PiGGS

more than she'd asked up Cecil R. Dupree. At least Ricky
had a little class and wouldn't jump her on the spot. He'd
ask a couple times, bring some more candy and see if she'd
spread out for that.

"It was my great pleasure that I have travel, had the
vacación, in the lovely German town and countryside in
the summer ago," Ricky said, looking about for a place to
set his coffee where Gloria wouldn't see. It was, truly, the
worst he'd ever tasted anywhere, even in San Angelo.

"Ah, we share an interest in that country, I believe.
Would I be correct in saying that?"

"What, I'm sorry." Gloria hadn't been listening at all,
though she liked the sort of sleepy, restful sound of Ricky's
voice, which was nice as Ricky Martin, better than Cheech
and Chong.

She'd been thinking about poor Jack, and the awful
thing Cecil had done, and it frightened her to think what
the crazy bastard might do next. Shoot, it might be anything at all, whatever crossed his mind. She knew things
Cecil had done, him and Grape and Cat, things she wished
she didn't know at all.

Ricky's words, though, suddenly cut through her
thoughts, and she looked at him and smiled, as if she'd
been there all along.

"You've been there? Really? I don't believe you ever
told me that."

"Oh, but yes. And I have not mentioned this thing to
you? Surely I have."

"No, now I'd remember that."

"Well then," Ricky said, settling uneasily in a
straightback chair that was clearly not designed for larger
men, and wobbled on the floor. Why in God's Holy Name,
he wondered, had the cunning German engineers made
this airplane of corrugation, like a fucking barn, like the

131

walls at Piggs. He wondered, too, what would happen if the ancient metal chose this moment to give way.

"I have seen Berlin, of course, this is a must on the list. But I spent much happy travel in the small towns as well. You are familiar with these towns, I imagine. I am guessing you have read about them and seen them on the television as well."

"Not any, I'm afraid. I guess I really should."

"But you speak the German tongue."

"Heavens no." Gloria had to laugh at that. "I don't speak any tongues at all."

"No? Well, then, allow me to say, Vas gestoppen der Gretel und Fritzen, grabben de clocken und der stein, miene hair? Vo sticken ein hosen und der Heinekins, go schleepin in der Benz."

"Wow." Gloria hugged her arms across her breasts. "What exactly did you *say* to me, Mr. Chavez? I hope it wasn't something foreign that isn't nice."

"No, no, no, Frawliner." Ricky clicked the heels of his gold-toed boots. "I said, 'Do you not think it is a cool evening here in Texas for the time of the year?' I think—if you will excuse the familiar, Miss Mundi, I said, 'you are a most kind and charming person.'"

"Now, I do not think you have to get into talk like that. Just say something else, like—okay, what you'd say if you were there, in one of those little towns you was talking about?"

"Yes, of course." Ricky leaned back and looked at the low, threatening ceiling overhead, and past Gloria Mundi to the black and ugly half of a weapon, which poked through the side of the plane. Earlier, Gloria had kindly pointed out that it was your standard, Beam-mounted 7.9 mm MG 15, on the starboard station.

"Ah yes," Ricky had said at that the time.

"I am recalling," he said now, "the charming, the *muy hermoso* villages such as Becks, Panzer, Schnitzel and Hans. Drinken is a favorite of mine. It rests in the foothills of the Fahrtwagen Mountains."

"I think I read about that."

"I expect you have indeed, Miss Mundi. It is quite a famous stop for the tourist person. They make clocks of the cuckoo, and a very nice wine."

"I wish I could go sometime. I'd like to go to see where they made the JU 52. It's on Daddy's tape, I ought to know it by now. I wish I could just *see* some of those places, instead of hearing about 'em all the time."

And, as she spoke, she leaned forward a bit, her back a slender bow, elbows on her knees, fingers dangling loose, her bare little toes picking at the corrugated floor.

Ricky Chavez felt a near desperate, overwhelming need, an ache, a longing for this lovely woman, a hunger that surpassed even physical desire, though he did not discount the nice pokies on her chest, the way her cutoffs vanished in the secret furrows between her torrid thighs, and, most certainly, he was entranced by the wondrous belly button that winked just below her T-shirt that read "Save the Badgers," which some fool had given her at Piggs.

Dios, he would give a hundred dollars, maybe up to three, simply to plant one kiss within that tiny hollow, possibly the finest innie he'd ever seen, except for that girl, whose name he could nearly recall, just south of Veracruz.

He became aware that these thoughts had partially set his loins afire, and turned, slightly, in his chair, to hide what Gloria Mundi might see, and find an improper display.

"The German nation of today," he went on quickly, "is a most pleasant place to be, for the peoples, they have not the savage nature of the past, and many now live fruitful lives, the same as you and I. The children and the grandchilds, I do not think they remember the bad things their country do to us before."

Gloria's manner, her posture and the alarming change taking place around her mouth, her throat, and, most especially in her eyes, had begun the moment Ricky Chavez embarked on his essay on the German people of today. Ricky, though, was so entranced with his new, and impressive fabrication of places he'd never seen, and a language no more familiar than Hindustani or Japanese, he missed the warning he should have seen.

"And what is *us?*" Gloria said, her jaw thrust out in a challenge that made Ricky blink. "Who is it *we* are talking about here? I don't recall any Germans bombing Acapulco or some other such town. You want to tell me what you're complaining about?"

Ricky was appalled. He felt the blood rush to his face. "I must tell you I was born in Laredo, Miss Mundi. I am an American, the same as you."

"Well *muy beano* for you. That's about half a block from that other Laredo, if I got my geography right."

"I—did not think you were of the racial persuasion. I regret to hear this is so."

"Is what's so?" Gloria stood so quickly Ricky stood as well, sending the straightback clattering to the floor. This woman was not overly tall without her stripper shoes, but anger seemed to add inches to her height.

"The way you talk, I thought you had a real feeling for the German people, an' I see that you don't. On the contraire, as the Frenchies like to say, you fucking don't like 'em at all."

"Please. You mistake my intent..."

"I know about your *intent*, mister, which is to stare at what I got inside my pants. I get enough of that at work, I sure don't need to put up with it here. And if you'd read your history careful, you'd know everyone in Germany wasn't all of the Hitler persuasion. Some of them fought 'cause that's the country where they was born. Just like some of our boys might have been Republican folks or someone from New York, that didn't stop them from defending their native land."

"This is—most certainly true," Ricky said, seeing all the progress he'd made fading before his eyes, thinking, now, he'd have to climb down the fucking ladder in the middle of the night, that he surely had no chance of staying up in the Junkers JU 52.

"The boy who flew this very airplane, who's name I will not mention to you, was just doing his duty to his country, and he had no part in the historic crimes of the National Social Party on people of other creeds."

Ricky looked at her. "Excuse me. How would you possibly know this was so?"

"And don't you approach me in a romantic manner anymore, and don't bring me any more shit. And this isn't because you're a Mescan, don't get the idea it is."

"Thank you. I appreciate that."

"You don't like my coffee you don't have to try and hide it somewhere."

"If you will try to accept my apology, Miss Mundi. Please. Der Straus verdancin is kaput, und der boaten is gesunk."

"An' what's that supposed to mean?"

"With all my heart, I beg that you—"

"Don't start, I don't need that kind of talk and I don't want it in German, either. Get out of my house, Mr. Chavez, before I get real pissed with you."

◆ ◆ ◆

Climbing down the shaky ladder with his eyes closed seemed to help, or would have, if he hadn't peeked to see if he was close to the ground.

Ricky was deeply upset. This was clearly a step back in his pursuit of Gloria Mundi. There would have to be new thought on the matter, an entirely new approach, which did not include candy or flowers. Possibly, this approach would not call for any of the normal practices of courtship at all.

Surely, it would have to include more in-depth research on the new Germany, and at least a basic understanding of the language.

"Dios! How is one supposed to know the fucking Krauts are as good as us now? When did they come up with that?"

23 TWENTY-THREE...

W hat he thought about was how it was before, how it was when things were going right, when things were going fine. There weren't that fucking many, like you had to take a day *off* to count them up or anything, it wouldn't take a lot of time.

In the movies, some jerk's thinking, he's thinking how it was in fifth grade, how he's riding on his bike, running through a bunch of leaves. It's always fucking autumn, the leaves are always falling off the trees.

The other thing is, there's a cute little chick, she's wearing this fuzzy sweater, her tits are just starting to grow, and the guy likes that, but he doesn't know what the hell to do. Dad's out mowing the lawn and the kid says "Hi!" and goes up to his room and jerks off, thinking about the pretty girl.

They don't ever show that, but that's what the kid's doing, you can bet your ass on that.

Jack can't think of any leaves. He can think about a bike but it's broken all the time. The thing he thinks about is riding in the Buick in Oklahoma City with the long-legged girl before the money from the job runs out. He thinks about a guy in a shit-kicker bar, the guy is built like a side of Kansas City beef, and Jack takes everything the guy can put out, then decks him with a left to the kidney and the guy sits down and cries.

There were four, maybe six other times. One had to do with drinking good whiskey, dropping a roll on the bar, buying drinks for the house. One had to do with another long-legged girl, this one in a trailer in Brazoria, Texas, a dirt-poor woman who had more class than the girl in the Buick, which happened sometimes.

And all those good times Jack could keep in a very small corner of his mind, they didn't take any room at all. What took up space, crowded everything out, was doing time in Huntsville, Texas, watching his gut go bad until it dried up all the mean he'd brought in from outside.

When that was gone the niggers and the spics and the Nazi fucking white trash remembered the tough guy they'd seen walk in, and were glad to see the fun times come around again.

◆ ◆ ◆

Jack wasn't mad at Cecil or even Grape or Cat. That was a lesson he'd learned in Huntsville too. All mad did was fuck up your head. Mad's the same as getting hot, an old con told him. Thinking, laying back, using your head, that's the same as being cool.

The guy who told him that was likely still there, but that didn't mean it wasn't true. What it meant was, crawling naked on the floor, everyone watching your dick bounce around didn't mean a thing now. It wasn't anything you could ever take back, play it right again. Lay back, be cool, you could think of something good, like punching out the big guy, riding with the long-legged girl. Fuck it, you did

138

that once, you could do it again, turn everything around, make it like it was before.

He still meant to kill Cecil R. Dupree, and Grape and Cat too. Pull a nice caper, get enough money to buy some good clothes, get a haircut, get some fine shoes. Shoes that didn't look like you played fucking nigger basketball.

Get on the good side of Gloria, the clothes would help with that. So would whacking Ricky Chavez, but he'd have to be careful, she'd really be pissed if she ever found out.

That's maybe four things to do, Jack thought, if you counted Cecil and his crew as just one. Four things is a lot, but what else did he have to do? Besides scrubbing pots and waiting tables in Piggs? Waiting for Rhino to think of some shit for him to do. You don't ever reach for something bigger than you are, you're never going to get a fucking star.

◆ ◆ ◆

He heard Grape walk up the stairs to Cecil's place, saw the dust drift from the cracks with each step he passed by.

He wasn't dozing off this time, he was wide awake now, and it didn't take any time at all to get where he wanted to go.

A concrete slab, one of the old cellar walls, had slots near the top where someone meant to put beams some-time. There were eight or ten slots Jack had found, wandering about the old dog pens with a flash. One of these was less than two feet beneath the boards of Cecil's floor.

It wasn't a comfortable perch, and your ass froze off on the cold concrete, but he didn't mind that. He could hear Cecil talk, hear him breathe, hear him on the john if you didn't stick your fingers in your ears.

Jack knew the two were drinking, you could hear the bottle click against the glass, you could smell the smoke from Cecil's cheap cigar.

Cecil wasn't happy, he was pissed, but there was nothing new about that.

"He says he's going to come, he better come," Cecil said. "Junior Ambrose wants to work with me, he better get a guy up here, stop fucking around."

"You heard what he said," Grape told him, "he said the guy was coming. Said he'd send him right away."

"Said he's comin' from where? He's coming from New Orleans, he's coming from fucking Mars?"

Grape laughed, and shook the ice in his glass. "Maybe Ambrose's kid, he's sending some guy got a little smarts. He isn't sending no Hutt Kenny this time, some asshole isn't smart enough to see if he's maybe got something shouldn't ought to be in his trunk.

"A guy don't check his car, a guy don't check his trunk, don't look under the hood, a guy like that's going to wind up in a dumpster somewhere, he's got no more smarts than that."

Grape felt he was on a roll now, that a story like this was worth telling twice, or maybe more than that.

"A guy like Kenny, he don't think about shit like that. He's thinking, he's thinking about Alabama Straight, what she's doing in his lap. He's thinking he gets back quick, he's got somebody that'll do that again. What he's thinking is—"

"I'm calling Junior. Fuck this."

"What, you mean now? You callin' him now?"

"What'd I say? I say, I'm calling him now, I'm calling him Easter, I'm calling him Christmas day?"

Jack could hardly hear Cecil's voice, even a few feet away, but when he started talking like that, you could figure the blood was pumping into his Lone Ranger face, turning it from cherry-red to black.

Grape, Jack knew, was aware of this too, because he wasn't real smartmouth now, he was talking extra quiet, like a yard guy maybe, or a waiter in a fancy restaurant.

"I was saying, what I was saying is it's awful late, Mr. Dupree, I don't give a fuck you're disturbing this guy, fuck him, he don't get to sleep all night. I'm thinking, an' you set me straight if I'm wrong, I'm thinking, even if the old man's kid he isn't too bright, he's maybe goin' to wonder, why is Mr. Dupree callin' in the middle of the night? Somethin's wrong up there, he's got somethin' on his mind, he's pulling some shit on me? I'm just sayin' what *he's* maybe thinking, I don't even know the guy's smart as that."

After a minute, Cecil said, "I think he's maybe not. I think he's a stupid fuck, or he wouldn't send someone like Kenny the Hutt up here to deal with me."

"I think you're absolutely right, Mr. Dupree—"

"I'm talking. I'm still talking, I'm saying maybe you're right, maybe the old man's watching the kid now, the kid screws up with Hutt. Maybe he's unretiring for a minute, even if his dick's falling off. I'm calling tomorrow. I'm calling after breakfast, I'm not calling Junior, I'm calling Ambrose, I'm talking to the old man myself. I'm—What? What's that, what you saying now?"

"I didn't say nothing, Mr. Dupree."

"You didn't say nothing, your face said something, okay? Guy's thinking something, he don't want to say it, that's what you're going to see, it's sitting on his face."

"Hey. It wasn't worth saying, I was thinking, you know, about Ambrose, what you said."

"The old man."

"Right, the old man. Not the kid, the old man."

"What?"

"Nothing, Mr. Dupree, I'm just saying, I'm saying up front, you know what you want to do, it's just what *I* was thinking, which don't mean shit, I'll say it anyway. I got to be straight, I don't feel good talking to Junior or the old man either one. I'm saying, don't give these fuckers nothing, like we give a shit about the buy or not. You don't show up, fuck you. There's lots of guys got merchandise, we'll get it somewhere else."

Cecil didn't answer at all. Jack hoped Grape was suffering, hoped he couldn't breathe, hoped his gut was knotting up. Grape was a cocky little bastard and mean as a snake, but he was scared of Cecil Dupree. Like anyone who had good sense knew Cecil didn't give a shit about anyone's opinion but his own.

"Where's Cat," Cecil said finally, "where's the dummy at?"

"You want him, I'll kick his ass, I'll get him up here."

"I don't want him, you don't want to kick his ass, you aren't as fucking dumb as that. Get me a couple Mars bars at the 7-'leven, I don't want a Mounds, I don't want a Milky Way, they don't got a Mars, you get it somewhere else."

"Yes, sir. Mars bars. You want me to get Cat go an' get a couple Mars bars, no Mounds, no—"

"I didn't say Cat, you hear me say Cat? You go, and take Cat with you. Get me a Dr Pepper too, they don't have that don't get me a fucking Pepsi, don't get me nothing at all."

"I'm on it," Grape said, "I think they got the Dr Pepper, I told the slope there last time we don't want to be drivin' all over the fucking county, we want him to keep 'em here."

"Do it," Cecil said. "Don't fucking talk about it, do it right now."

◆ ◆ ◆

142

PIGGS

Jack listened to Grape stomp down the stairs, saw his motion through the cracks. In a minute, he heard Cat growling somewhere, then they both were gone.

Jack's back hurt and his legs had gone numb, but he didn't want to move, it was much too quiet up there. Cecil didn't even know he had a cellar under Piggs, and Jack didn't want to tell him now.

Jack tried to rub some feeling in his legs, but he couldn't reach far. Cecil hadn't moved, hadn't breathed as far as Jack could tell. How long did it take to go to the store and back? Ten, fifteen minutes. Maybe ten inside, fifteen back. Two, carry your four...

Cecil moved. The floor creaked when he stalked across the room, bare feet slapping against the floor. He stopped, somewhere to Jack's right. The lock clicked loudly in the door. Clicked once, clicked twice again. Jack had never been in Cecil's rooms, but the locks were no surprise. A gangster of Cecil's stature would want some good locks on the door.

Cecil turned on the TV. It sounded like an all-night movie. Jack thought it might be *Ben Hur*. Man, that chariot race was something else again. They used to show it in Huntsville all the time. The cons would bet on it, and try to kill each other if their guy didn't win.

Cecil moved across the room. Walked right up above Jack, then stopped. Jack felt the hairs stand up on his neck. Cecil couldn't see him, couldn't guess he was there, but that didn't help at all. Your person of the criminal persuasion could see things regular people couldn't see. Crooks and cops, they could both do that. Jack wished he had some of that extra-sensitive power himself, but he'd never been that good.

Cecil squatted down. The floorboards squeaked, letting in a tiny speck of light. It sounded like Cecil was pry-ing up the floor. Jack held his breath. Cecil was doing something, just past the concrete wall, where Jack couldn't see. And he didn't have to pry, the boards just sort of rolled free.

Cecil lifted something out. Set it down right above Jack. Another click, another lock. Jack listened, pressed his ear closer to the boards by his head.

A new sound now, a sound like leaves, a whispery, rustly kind of sound. *Slick-slick—slick.* A crinkle then a snap. A really pleasant sound, nice as it could be. A sound like that could help a person sleep real good...

It struck, him, then, and Jack made a little sound himself, and cut it off quick. Money. That's what it was. Holy shit, Cecil Dupree was counting his money, a whole box full!

Slick-slick-slick. Big, stubby Cecil fingers rifling through the bills. A stack went *plop!* on the floor, and then another after that.

How high could you go before a stack fell? You wouldn't keep them all in one stack, you'd do a different stack, maybe a different stack for different bills. Cecil wouldn't bother with ones, so they had to be big. Twenties and hundreds, Jack guessed. Your crime boss, even if he lived in Mexican Wells, wouldn't want to mess with little bills. They'd be in little stacks, then, with paper strips around them, or maybe rubber bands. All you had to do was count a stack, you wouldn't have to—

Jack almost fell off his perch. Grape hit the stairs, three at a time, Cat pounding on his heels, a gorilla, Godzilla, a buffalo in heat.

Just above Jack, the stacks hopped quickly back in the box, and the box disappeared.

"Hey, Mr. Dupree?" Grape said, rattling the knob, "I can't get in, I think the thing's locked."

Cecil clicked the locks, opened the door.

"What you got it locked for, Mr. Dupree? Why you lockin' the door?"

"'Cause you don't got any manners, asshole, you or Cat either one. You knock from now on, you don't come walking in, you show a little respect, act like you—What's that, what the fuck you got there? If that's a fucking Mounds, you bring me something with coconut in it, you're headed back to the 7-'leven store."

"They didn't have nothing else, Mr. Dupree."

"That's what they had," Cat said, "they didn't have nothing else."

"Shut up. Shut the fuck up."

Cecil grabbed the sack from Grape. "Don't bother coming in, you're going back out. I'm thinking, I'm thinking this Mescan, this Ricky whatever, he's hanging around, he's messing with the girls. I don't want him in Piggs. What it is, I don't want him *any*where. Do I got to explain this to you or what?"

"No sir, you sure don't. I don't like him, he's all the time, like you said, messing with the girls. He comes in tomorrow, me and Cat, we'll take care of the guy—"

"No. You won't." Cecil poked a finger in Grape's chest.

"You don't fuck with the guy in Piggs. You don't do nothing here. The guy's got a condo in San Antone. He's in the book. You do it there."

"Right. First thing tomorrow, we'll get on it, me an' Cat."

"Now."

"What?"

"Get in the fucking car, no you can't take the Cad. Get in the car, take care of it now."

"It's the middle of the night," Cat said.

"How the fuck do you know? You can't tell time, how you know it's the middle of the night?"

"We'll get right on it," Grape said.

"I appreciate that."

"You going to call Mr. Ambrose, you still thinkin' on that?"

Cecil didn't answer. He slammed the door in Grape's face.

Jack heard the pair move back down the stairs, a great deal slower than when they'd come up.

Cecil opened the fridge, shut it up again. Sat down, turned up the TV. It was still *Ben Hur*. With all the commercials, that was a real long show.

Jack climbed down, got to the floor before the numb went out, didn't care about the pain, he was too full of anger to care if he broke a leg.

Son of a bitch, fucking Cecil Dupree! He wasn't happy embarrassing people, making them crawl buck naked with an underage singer on their back. Now he had to kill Ricky Chavez, take that away from Jack too.

That's the way people were, the way they'd always been, as long as Jack could recall. You want something, someone else wants it too. They get there first, there's nothing left for you.

"Well fuck you, Cecil," Jack said aloud. "I hope you miss the end of *Ben Hur,* I hope you choke on your fucking Dr Pepper too..."

TWENTY-FOUR...

Jack woke with scratchy eyes. Bloodshot, gritty eyes, glued up tight. Eyes stuck solid with some kind of shit your body made just for that effect.

Why? Jack wondered. Why would it want to do that? Your body made lots of other yuck. Little white things at the corner of your mouth. Snot for your nose, wax for your ears.

Snot was okay if you were six. It wasn't any fun after that.

Wax was okay, it could help you pass the time. You could bend a paper clip, stick it in your ear. See how much you got. Sometimes you got a little, sometimes you got a lot. Guys in the joint would bet on wax. Not the same guys who bet on *Ben Hur*. This was a different bunch of guys.

Jack rubbed the crust out, sat up and looked around. Ahmed sprawled on bags of rice across the storage room. Ahmed was asleep or maybe not. It was hard to tell if you didn't close your eyes. Where he came from, Ahmed said, you keep your eyes open all the time.

Jack hoped the raghead was dozing now. It was almost light, and Jack knew he'd only had half an hour's sleep. If Ahmed had seen him come in, he'd ask where he'd been all night. Jack would make something up and he wasn't good at that. Everyone he knew could lie like a dog, but it didn't work for him. One look and you knew. This was not a good trait for someone of the outlaw persuasion, but there was nothing Jack could do.

◆ ◆ ◆

Ahmed didn't ask. Rhino did. Rhino walked in with a chicken from the fridge. First thing he said was, "What the fuck you up to, Jack, you was out all night."

"Woo-woo," Ahmed said, and shot Jack a nasty wink, "I t'ink Jhack, he is getting heem a little, this is what I t'ink."

"Anybody asking you, Ary-fat?" Rhino peered around the kitchen with his ball-bearing eyes. "Anyone ask this sand nigger something, I didn't hear?"

Rhino split the chicken down the middle. Jack twitched as the cleaver dug wood. Ahmed was good with a cleaver, but Rhino had arms as big as Ahmed's waist.

Ahmed found something to stir. Ortega found a broom and swept his way out the back door.

"I couldn't sleep," Jack said. "I walked around a while."

"Uh-huh. An' where'd that be?"

"Nowhere. Walking is all."

"All night. Walking somewhere."

"No sir, not all the time. Sometimes, sometimes I sat down a while."

"Not all the time. Sometimes, you was sitting for a while. Sometimes—"

"Rhino, that's what I said, I was walking, that's all, I was just—"

148

In the dread, awful silence, Jack could hear a fly fart on the screen door, hear the paint peeling off the wall.

Rhino looked at Jack. Looked at his hands. Wiped chicken on his apron, looked at Jack again.

"That was a shameful thing to do, what Cecil did. Isn't no way to treat a white man, don't care what he done. What the fuck you looking at, Sodum *Hoo*-sayn? All you mothers get moving back here, I got a Chink restaurant to run..."

TWENTY-FIVE...

Jack thought he ought to feel bad, but he felt a lot better than he had in some time. You lose a little sleep, you can do without that. But it wasn't every day you could hear Rhino say something bad about Cecil R. Dupree. That was something else, and letting you smart off a little, too.

"I am glahd I live to see these t'ing," Ahmed said. "Dhis is like you standin' in the strit, a comit is falling, the comit don' hit you, hit ever'body else. It is like you peekin' in the window, there is a naked movie stahr. There is Jhulias Robers, she got no close on at all. Both of these t'ing, you never be t'inkin' they goin' to hoppen to you."

"I don't want to talk about this," Jack said. "I don't want to discuss it, so just get it out your head."

"Hey, I don' blame you for these. I am jus' saying, mahn—"

"Yeah, well don't. Don't say nothing, that's all I want to hear about that."

"If I was you," Ortega said, "I'd put the incident out of my head, and never look at it again."

151

Ortega's eyes were slightly out of whack. He'd seen Jack's encounter with Rhino the day before as a miraculous event, and had not expected to see it again. He had gone to his car and downed a half pint of El Escorpión, a brand of *mescal* so bad it was scorned by vagrants on the street.

"Dhot is no makin' any sense," Ahmed said. "Once a t'ing is being in you haid, it is stickin' in dere, man, is not comin' out again."

"This is what the Ay-rab people are thinking," Ortega said. "The Ay-rab and the Jew. No one else is thinking that."

"Ha! A Mescan, he is tellin' me this? I am listen to a Mescan who is drinkin' cactus piss? I am not be listen to this."

"An Ay-rab is the flea on the dick of the dog. You insult my country, you don't even have the good sense to eat a pig."

"Pig is for the Satan's people to eats. God is tellin' you that. You don' know, you don' know these?"

Jack didn't hear any more, he was out of the kitchen, out the back door and down the street, the fire inside him heating up again, the pipes pumping battery acid so fast he could scarcely stay on his feet.

He clutched at his gut, the agony pulling at his features, soaking him with sweat. Shit, it hadn't been that bad since—what? Not even the horsey business had hit him like this. It was those two gabbing, is what it was. The whole country was full of assholes from foreign lands. What were they doing here, why didn't they go the fuck away?

Jack walked out past Wan's and sat beneath the big live oak where Ortega parked his car. It wasn't even eight or nine, but the sun was hot enough to start the insects buzzing in the trees.

PIGGS

He knew it wasn't Ahmed or Ortega or Rhino either that had set his belly on a spree. What it was, was what you call your relayed reaction, which meant your emotions and shit were catching up with your bodily parts and giving 'em hell.

He had tried to shove all that aside, what happened, what he'd done. It had scared him so much he could hardly believe it was him that had done it at all.

Ahmed didn't know it, but was dead right about that. Once you had stuff in your head, wasn't any way to shove it out again.

It had happened, and it wouldn't go away. Just like all the other crap he'd done in his life: You can't take anything back. It's always there, whether you like it or not.

◆ ◆ ◆

He got through the morning, doing all the things he'd put off the week before. When he had to go in the kitchen, Ahmed and Ortega pretended he wasn't there. Rhino was out front yelling at the guy from Tex Savallo's, who'd brought the wrong meat the second time this week.

Wan's never opened til five, and there wasn't any crowd at Piggs. Only two dancers were on, Laura Licks and Whoopie LaCrane. Both of them shuffled around the stage like the girls in *Naked Zombie Wives,* which Ahmed had rented six or eight times.

Cecil was nowhere in sight, and neither was Grape or Cat. In a way, Jack was grateful for that, but it was sort of like waiting for the other shoe to drop, and it didn't help the fire in his gut.

◆ ◆ ◆

You never know when something's going to happen, when you're going to know something you didn't know before, when it's going to pop right into your head.

Which is why Jack was so startled when it happened, he almost dropped a case of Shiner Beer. It hit him right there, out of nowhere at all. He knew, at once, exactly what the money in Cecil's stash was for, and couldn't imagine why he hadn't seen it clearly before.

The thought brought such a happy grin, he was glad nobody was around. It wasn't an ordinary stash up there, it was money put aside, money for the dope buy from Ambrose Junior, and *that* meant Jack would be a whole lot richer when he stole it, richer than he'd dreamed about before...

TWENTY-SIX...

Jack had a box he kept in the corner, back behind the ten-gallon drums of Lotus Dream Soy from Wichita, Kansas, and the Shanghai Noodles from Maine. There was very little in the box except Tylenol and Xanax and Pepcid-AC and wintergreen Tums, and half a dozen other remedies he'd tried. None of them stopped the rage in his belly, even if you took the whole bunch at one time.

There was a pretty nice tie some dude had left at Wan's. A letter, he'd found in the street, from someone in France. Jack couldn't read it, but with the letter was a photo of a middle-aged guy in nothing but a Panama hat, so Jack guessed what the letter was about.

There were two other things in the box, paperbacks he'd found in the Greyhound station in Ada, Oklahoma. Jack had never read either one, but he was certain the books, found together like that, held some meaning he was meant to understand.

He took all the Pepcid-AC and the Tums and the rest of the Tylenol, and went to the kitchen, where Ahmed had orders waiting for Piggs. Recycled egg rolls, and buffalo wings with the Chef's Special Sauce. Ahmed put certain desert powders in the sauce he said would sterilize the Caucasian race. As soon as everyone in America ate at Wan's, that would be the end of that.

◆ ◆ ◆

Jack's gut had been hurting all day, hurting all the night before. Now that darkness was on him again, primal magma spewed from the earth, churned, burned and boiled at such a fierce and awesome heat, it was all Jack could do to keep from dropping everything, writhing on the ground.

He was frightened, scared out of his wits. The thing he'd set in motion now filled him with dread. Some other Jack must have done it, not him—some Jack who'd lost his fucking mind.

"The best thing to do," he told himself, spilling egg rolls in his wake, "is to walk out back and down the road, get to 35 and hitch a ride, and don't come back again."

◆ ◆ ◆

Someone said hello. It might have been Laura, it might have been Minnie, he couldn't tell which. He had to see Gloria, had to talk to her, and he couldn't do that. She'd see the whole thing, see it in his face, plain as the ten o'clock news.

Halfway through Piggs, he saw the college dudes again. The trucker guy, the one who'd been a horsey the night before, had brought along some friends.

From the shadows near the bar, he risked a look at Cecil's table. Cecil was alone, no one else was there, just Cecil R. Dupree, no shirt, no shoes, just bib overalls. He was bent nearly over the table, tearing at a rib, ripping off the meat, spitting out the gristle, tossing the bones on the floor. Now and then he drew a thick hand across his face, wiping the sauce on his pants.

As Jack stood in shadow, stood there and watched, Cecil stopped and froze, a rib in midair, jerked up straight, so fast, so quick, Jack was certain those razor-black eyes had caught him, found him and pinned him to the wall.

Then the eyes shifted, found a target to the right, squeezed into tiny little slits. The lavender mask turned purple, then solid bloody black.

Grape and Cat came through the door that led to Wan's, three feet from Jack. They didn't look at Jack, didn't know he was there. Didn't look at Cecil, either, and Jack knew why, knew where they'd been, why they were back.

He was caught, in that moment, somewhere between desperation, diarrhea, and the exquisite sense of being totally alive. He was either James Bond or fucking Pee-wee Herman, and, for an instant, his belly didn't hurt at all...

TWENTY-SEVEN...

The greaser wasn't home, Mr. Dupree, that's what I'm saying, that's the God's truth, we was there all night, the guy don't come, the fucker's not home."

"He wasn't home," Cat said. "Fucker's not home."

Cecil looked at Cat, looked at Cat a while and gripped the table till his fingers turned white.

"You tell me somethin' *he's* telling me, you tell me somethin' twice, you do that again I'm burning your dirty magazines, I'm cutting off your foot."

"I'm sorry. I'm real sorry, Mr. Dupree."

"You're sorry as you can be, Cat. You're no good for nothing I can see."

Cat wanted to cry. When Cecil got after him for something, he was scared he might crack, shatter into little pieces like they did on the cartoon shows sometimes. Cat wondered how they did that, how you could do that and be okay again.

"How you know he wasn't in there," Cecil said, making the two stand, like you make kids do, they go to see the principal, showing these clowns he was too pissed to let them sit down.

"You go in, you check the place out, the guy's not hidin' under the bed somewhere?"

"They got alarms, Cec—Mr. Dupree. It's all wired up, it's a nice part of town."

"They got a garage?"

"Every condo, they got a garage, it's built in."

"The Mescan got a car in there?"

"You can't see in. You gotta have a beeper you want to get in."

"Fuck, you dropped it, Grape, that's what you did. I ask you do somethin' easy, you fucking drop it, you come back to me and feed me shit like this. A guy, he's got a security thing, he's got it so it whoopas you come inna door, it isn't on every fucking window, guy's got a half-ass lock on the door out back.

"You dropped it, Grape. I am very disappointed you are dropping somethin' like this. The taco, I'm thinking he's up in his bed, his car's inna garage, you and the dummy here are riding round the fucking block, you're eatin' burgers and fries."

"We didn' have no fries," Cat said.

"Mr. Dupree," Grape said, "I got to say, an' I'm saying this in all respect, you're not being fair about this. It isn't right, the guy's not there, I'm not wrong about that, the guy is *not* in the house—"

"Get me a couple Coors. Get 'em from the back where it's cold. Don't open them or nothin', bring 'em here."

Grape didn't argue, didn't let it show, knew why Cecil was giving him this gofer job instead of Cat. Didn't give a shit, now, didn't care. You want a couple beers, asshole? Fine, good old fuckin' Grape, he's bringing you couple beers. Fuckin' Grape don't forget about that...

◆ ◆ ◆

"You can sit," Cecil said to Cat, "sit, don't talk, you talk you drive me fuckin' nuts."

"Okay, Mr. Dupree."

"You hear what I said?"

"Yes, sir. Don't talk, you drive me fuckin' nuts."

"I give up, forget it. Shit, you already forgot, right?"

Cecil looked around the room, checked the list he carried in his head, checked the crowd, checked the bar, knew, in a blink, which bartender was sweetening a drink for a friend, what girls were letting some big spender cop an extra feel. He could tell, to the nickel, to the dime, who was goofing off, who was stealing him blind.

"What's wrong with Grape? Why's he acting like that? I chew the guy out, he's giving me a look. I don't like it, he's giving me a look like that."

He was talking to Cat, but Cat didn't hear. Cecil had told him not to talk, he was off on Neptune somewhere.

Thinking on it now, Cecil wished he'd held off on Grape for a while. He counted on Grape, and Grape knew it, and he'd hit him heavy on the Chavez deal, because he was pissed Grape hadn't pulled it off. Fucking beaner in his fancy clothes, hitting on Gloria all the time, that shit had to stop. The girl was hard enough to nail without some Mescan feeding her a lot of crap.

Now he was going to have to tell Grape he was wrong on something else, that a call to Ambrose was looking like a good idea. Not a *good* idea, fuck that, but something maybe had to be done to get the buy off the ground.

The thing was, he wanted to work with this bunch because they had the connections, had the merchandise, and were smart about the business, in spite of this moron Kenny or Hutt or whatever the fuck, and Cecil had the

161

outlets, knew how to make money on the stuff without getting close to the street end himself.

Okay, the two stiffs in the trunk, the Ambrose guys could maybe take offense, you had to give 'em that. It wasn't on purpose, and didn't mean any disrespect, but you could take it like that, which Cecil figured was the reason these assholes were holding up the game.

So they made their point, and that's enough of that. Now, the disrespect's the other way, it's coming at Cecil R. Dupree, and Cecil isn't sitting still for that.

"I'm not sitting still for that," he told Grape, as Grape delivered the beers, bringing two for Cecil and two for himself.

Cecil acted like nothing had happened, like he always did, you had to go along with that.

"I'm calling, I'm telling New Orleans get a guy up here, get him here tomorrow, day after that, or forget it, we're buying from somebody else."

"That's the thing to do," Grape said, "I gotta agree with that. Those guys are messing with us now."

"You think I'm right in this."

"Yes sir, I surely do."

"Good. I'm glad you're not saying this because I'm pissed about the greaser thing. You make it right, I'm okay with that."

"Consider it done, Mr. Dupree."

Cecil looked at Grape a long time, waiting for Grape to look away, but Grape held on, didn't look funny in the eye or anything, he looked okay.

"I got no grief on this, we're okay, you get the thing done."

"I appreciate it, Mr. Dupree."

"Cecil. You can do Cecil again, I don't tell you something else."

"Me too, Mr. Dupree," Cat said.

"Me too what?"

"What he said. What Grape did."

Cecil said, "Get us a couple more beers. Get yourself a big orange. Get some fucking peanuts over here."

"Sure, Mr. Dupree."

Cat stood, rose up like a grizzly, like a mountain, like a tree, blocking out the light, the bar, Minnie Mouth and Alabama Straight, the southern end of Piggs.

It always aggravated Cecil, always caused him to wonder how a person so big, a person with the strength of a Cape buffalo, could have the brains of a brick. The guy's head alone, there was room in there for two, three brains to spare. Instead, there were only instructions how to walk, how to shit. How to tell which is a banana, which is a fish.

Every time he asked Cat to get something for him, Cecil wished he'd sent Grape, or done it himself. The agony, the effort, the dreadful confusion that overwhelmed Cat was a terrible thing to see.

Cecil watched him coming back, watched him mouth the words, trying, with fierce determination, to hang onto them before they simply drifted away.

"beer...big orange...fucking peanuts..."

Good, doing fine, the dummy remembered what to get, remembered where to bring them back.

Then, as Cecil watched, some neural lint, some static from outer space, twisted Cat's features into awesome disarray. Something scrambled the tortured process in his head, derailed his train, tossed him off the track.

"Orange," Cat said..."beer...fucking peanuts... nigger...beer...fucking orange...nigger...fucking beer..."

"Huh?" Cecil blinked, squinted his tiny eyes, certain, now, Cat's cheap wiring was shorting out.

"What you talkin' about, what's the matter with you?"

Cat didn't answer, didn't have to try. Someone appeared, someone walked past the giant into view. White

163

shirt, white tie, pearl-gray suit, purple shades and silver shoes. Cool, slick, six-foot-eight, black as blackest night.

"Mr. Cecil R. Dupree," the man said, smooth as ice cream, fine as peach pie, "I am Hamilton Taylor Gerrard, and I represent Mr. Ambrose Junior of New Orleans, who would like to offer you a fair, square and honest business deal..."

TWENTY-EIGHT...

This is a criminal act that you are doing, you are in the very deep trouble, my friend. When you are detaining a person this is a most illegal matter for which the penalty is severe.

"However, I am willing to look upon this as a grave misunderstanding, possibly a humor, a joke of some kind. If you agree to be releasing me at once, I would even consider a modest reward."

Jack pretended he wasn't paying any mind, but he was. Looking the other way, like cleaning your fingernails, doing something else, what that did was demoralize your captive, in a psychological way. This was a proven technique, used by agents of many nations, and the cops in Dallas and Oklahoma City, two cities he knew about for sure.

"You are fucking through, Mr. Chavez?" Jack said finally.

"If you're finished talking, you can shut your lip an' listen to me. You don't want to do that, I'll leave you here and you can yell through the stomping and the stereo up there an' someone'll come and let you go, they ever figure where the hell you are, which by the way don't anybody know."

"I will not yell or shout," Ricky said. "I do not feel this would help the matter at all. I would like to deal with you directly on this matter, Jack. I think we can come to the *solución,* the answer that will satisfy your needs."

"You ought to thank me, is what you ought to do. You'd be a cold burrito if it wasn't for me. You can believe that or not, it don't matter to me."

Ricky supposed, in a most peculiar way, this was so. It was not impossible to believe the gringo mobster with the Lone Ranger face would kill him, simply because he wished to have relations of an intimate nature with the lovely Gloria Mundi. Possibly, he dared imagine, relations of a more permanent nature than that.

On the other hand, Jack had made it clear his rescue was for the purpose of dispatching Ricky himself. This, to Ricky's mind, took some of the air out of Jack's noble act.

Ricky did not think Jack was a *loco,* a person of the nut persuasion, in the sense that Cecil could be said to truly be crazy as shit. Jack was more of the cunning nature, of the sly, lacking in manners and *cultura* of any sort. Not so much evil in the heart as a lack of reason in the head.

Still, if a man is tied naked except for his boots, lying on the concrete floor in the pen of the dogs, the difference in the Cecils and the Jacks of the world is of little matter at the time. What matters is how to avoid the dying in such a wretched place.

◆ ◆ ◆

He remembered most of it now. Climbing down the shaky ladder from the Junkers airplane in the tree. Then *bop!* on the head, and he's in somebody's trunk, someone else's, not his. He is in a car where the exhaust travels directly through the trunk and out a ragged hole in the back. Ricky recalls little after that.

If anything is more humiliating that his naked condition, it's the sight of his possessions Jack has laid out neatly on the floor. His clothing, his Patek Philippe, his Cordovan leather wallet from Spain, two very nice rings of silver, sixteen-hundred dollars, and a number of credit cards.

Under the seat of his car, Jack has also found his .357 silver-plated Colt Magnum, with the Mexican eagle and serpent engraved on the weapon, and the gold *pesos* inlaid on the ivory grip.

In his jacket, Jack has found the damning evidence of condoms from France. This, Ricky fears, could seal his fate with Jack, who knows the occasion for which they were intended. More than once, Jack has let his flashlight shine in an accidental manner on Ricky's private parts. And, for the first time in his life, Ricky Chavez is grateful they are not spectacular, but only of normal size for his weight and height.

"You gotta understand," Jack said, leaning against the chain link side of the pen, studying Ricky's fine watch, "this is a personal thing with me, it don't have no racial undertones. I don't care for beaners, or any of your swarthy-colored types, but this has got nothing to do with that. This has to do with trying to fuck Gloria Mundi, and I won't put up with that."

"I admit to an admiration for this woman," Ricky said, hesitating a moment to collect his thoughts, "I will not deny that. But what you speak of I resent, for you are painting my intentions as *soez,* ordinary and coarse."

"Yeah, well coarse is as coarse does, I'm not going into that. I don't want you messin' with Gloria. Her and I isn't some passin' affair, we intend to settle down."

Ricky was glad the light was off his face at the time, for he was quite amazed to learn this.

"I was truly not aware of such a thing. Miss Mundi has never mentioned that to me."

"That's because it isn't your business, Mr. Chavez. It's nothing you need to know."

"Yes. I see."

"Good. I'm fucking happy you do."

"And you feel—because I have shown my affection to this lady as well, you must murder me in cold blood, this is so?"

"You embarrassed or anything, I could find something to cover you up. I'm not a mean-spirited person, Mr. Chavez. I'd say having too kindly a nature has been a weakness in me, and likely done more harm than good."

"A blanket of some manner would be appreciated, yes. And I must complain these restraints are uncomfortably tight."

"That's your ordinary duct tape, is all. It won't cut your blood off, it'll give."

Jack paused to listen as the bozos upstairs began to cheer and stomp, and a fine veil of dust descended through the cracks. The DJ put on "God Save the Queen," which meant Maggie Thatch was coming on, and Gloria would be up after that.

He looked at Ricky's very fine watch and wondered what it cost. Likely more than his Buick Park Avenue, which Jack had left where he'd found it, in a brushy turn-around near the **BATTLE OF BRITUN FAMILY FUN PARK.** The watch was hard to read, even with a flash. It had little diamonds for numbers, which irritated Jack no end. If he was right, it was half past one.

"I've had some thought on this since last night, Mr. Chavez, which might be of interest to you. It's possible—

and I don't say it'll happen that way—that you could be a help to me, which means I'd be keeping you alive."

"I would be most interested in being of help to you, Jack."

"Yeah, I'm not surprised to hear that. The thing is, Cecil Dupree has got a box full of money up in his place, which is right above Piggs. I don't know exactly how much, but it's a lot. Cecil's going to make a drug buy with that dough. Someone's coming up soon from the Ambrose bunch in New Orleans. In case you don't know, that's a mob empire down there, a lot of whose members have been cited on network TV.

"What I am saying is, I'm going to get that money for myself. It isn't legal, it comes from criminal enterprise, so it isn't stealing like you hold up a store. I intend to use it for good, which is to start a new life for myself, and take Gloria away from all this."

Ricky hoped his feelings would not betray him. In the motion pictures, persons of the Hispanic nature were either highly agitated, foaming at the mouth, or appeared to be drugged, with no expression at all. At the moment, it was the clown, the *payaso,* holding up an adobe wall, that Ricky wished Jack to see.

"That is a most ambitious and truly daring idea, Jack. I have no experience in the robbery trade, but I should be pleased to be of service in any way I can..."

"Put a lid on the kiss-ass stuff, *amigo,* I don't need none of that. An' I don't need help on the job, either. It's your kind of stealing where I can use a little advice."

Ricky shook his head. "I do not see what I can do. I am in the banking business, Jack."

"Right. That's what I'm talking about. Big time crooks, your white shirt stuff. I get the money, you hide it. All but a little running money, the rest in like an overseas off-shore truss."

"Yes," Ricky said, "I can do that."

"Good. Then you got a fair chance of remaining among the living, Mr. Chavez."

"I am honored to work with you, Jack."

"Fuck you are. Just don't get any fancy greaser ideas. I've seen 'bout every Ricardo Montalban picture twice..."

TWENTY-NINE...

Cecil R. Dupree had spoken to a number of niggers up close, but never one exactly like this. If Hamilton T. Gerrard had ever pushed a lawn mower in his life, it didn't show now.

Cecil's first thought, his primal reaction, was to shoot this uppity bastard on the spot. Not a real good idea, with a couple hundred customers around. That, and if he really came from Ambrose, Cecil needed to hear what he had to say. You could always shoot a guy later, you didn't have to do it right away.

"First thing is," said Hamilton T. Gerrard, "is a message from Mr. Ambrose Junior himself. Mr. Ambrose like to say he harbor no ill feelings regarding the mishap what occurred in connection to Mr. Hutt Kenny's visit up here. That is water below the bridge. Mr. Ambrose say an accident like that might happen once, but odds are it wouldn't likely happen again. You understand what I'm saying, Mr. Dupree?"

"Yeah. Give Mr. Ambrose Junior my personal regards. Tell him I don't forsee any mishaps like that. Tell him the odds are good he won't be sending another asshole with funny-looking shirts up here."

Hamilton Gerrard grinned. "I will tell him just that, Mr. Dupree. I know he'll be pleased. You gentlemen mind if I sit? I am cursed with abnormal height, and I can barely see y'all down there."

"Please do," Cecil said, and decided he would shoot Mr. Gerrard in the knees first. That would take care of any fucking problem with abnormal height.

"Welcome to Piggs, Mr. Gerrard. Let me get you something to drink."

"I believe I'll decline right now, but I am grateful for the thought. Now, Mr. Dupree, here is what Mr. Ambrose Junior suggests that we do. I have brought the merchandise in the quantity you discussed with Mr. Ambrose some time ago."

"No partials," Cecil said. "We do the whole thing, I told him that."

"And he agrees, sir, you'll be pleased to hear. That's a gesture of goodwill on Mr. Ambrose' part. The price, now, that'll be seventy-five. And if you are looking surprised, Mr. Dupree, and I believe that's what I see, Mr. Ambrose thought the extra ten might serve as a gesture of goodwill on *your* part, you see."

"I see where Mr. Ambrose Junior is going, and with all due respect, fuck him. I'll go five for goodwill, if Mr. Ambrose will agree to go back to sixty-five the next time we do a deal."

"Mr. Ambrose Junior discuss that with me, and he say because he hold you in highest regard, he accept the extra five, and he guarantee the price stay at the figure next time."

For a long moment, Cecil R. Dupree and Hamilton T. Gerrard held one another in a cold and penetrating gaze. Neither one blinked, neither gave an inch, both of them willing to die before they'd look away. Then, each man gave the very slightest of nods to the other, and each sat back in his chair.

"This is Grape here, and that's Cat," Cecil said. "You make the trip up here yourself, or you bring some company along?"

"I get lonesome, I ride by myself."

Cecil grinned at that, and Grape did too. Cat simply stared, as he had from the moment this strange, exotic creature had walked into his world. Cat knew there were people who were black, he'd seen them lots of times. But Cat kept things in order in his head, he knew where things belonged, where they ought to be. Cars were in the street, they weren't up in the sky. Soda pop was orange or brown, it never was blue. Niggers were *outside* of Piggs, they never were in. Only one was in now, and that hurt Cat's head.

"Don't mind him," Cecil said, "he don't have a big social agenda, he don't get out a lot. He doesn't mean any disrespect for persons of the colored persuasion. We just don't get a lot of your people in here."

"I didn't notice," said Mr. Gerrard. "Not a lot of light in here."

"That's part of the illusion and all. Guys come in, it's private, don't anyone know they're here. But I expect you've been in a place like this before."

Mr. Gerrard smiled. "I've got 1:43, Mr. Dupree. I'd be pleased if we could take care of our business at four. Outside. I'll have my package, you'll have yours."

Mr. Gerrard stood, unfolding his skinny frame up to a full six-nine.

"Four's kinda late," Cecil said. "We close up at three. Three-thirty's better for me."

"Persons of the colored persuasion stay up all night sometimes, Mr. Dupree."

Before Cecil could answer, Hamilton T. Gerrard had smiled once more and walked away.

"Pow," Cecil said. He cocked his finger and fired again. "Pow, motherfucker, your black ass is dead."

"The guy's tall," Grape said. "You got to give him that."

"They're supposed to be tall, you dope. A short guy, how's he going to play basketball...?"

THIRTY...

This is not right, Jack. I have agreed to help you in your robbery enterprise. We are working together, my friend. You do not treat a person who is doing the cooperation with you in such a manner as this."

"Mr. Chavez, shut the fuck up. We aren't working together, and we sure aren't friends. You're doing what I tell you 'cause that's what you gotta do."

Ricky didn't answer, and that was fine with Jack. The guy was irritating, talking all the time. Which is what your Mescan's doing, that's what he's got to do. A taco don't talk a lot is fine. You get a good Mescan boxer, he's hell in the ring, he don't talk all the time. Same thing with your black sports figures, they can beat a white guy coming and going, on the field or in the ring. Jack didn't know why, but it was so.

He couldn't blame Chavez for being pissed. Crawling out the cellar up the hole has got to be pure aggravation, a guy's stark naked, his hands taped up, that's got to be a bitch.

Now the guy's really complaining, he's triple-duct-taped to the dumpster back of Wan's, his ankles taped too, taped around his gold-tipped boots, Jack figured he'd be pissed too.

"I got to put this stuff on your mouth, an' there'll be some discomfort in that. It's for your protection, though, in case you start yelling or something, it's Cecil or one of them that's coming, and you don't want that."

"That is not necessary. I will not call out."

"I know you think you won't now. But I seen panic set in when you least expect it to."

"I will not lie to you, Jack. I intend to keep my end of our agreement, but that does not mean I do not hold you in contempt. I think you are a *puerco* of the very worst kind."

"Whatever that is, I don't expect it's any good. And I wouldn't respect you, Mr. Chavez, if you didn't resent the treatment you've received."

"That revolver has sentimental value to me. The watch does not, but it is very expensive as you can see."

"Right. You hang in there, Mr. Chavez, you going to be just fine."

Before Ricky could speak again, Jack wrapped the duct tape across his mouth, stretching it around his head twice. Ricky didn't move, but he had much to say with his eyes, which Jack thought were hostile at best.

◆ ◆ ◆

Ortega's car was where it ought to be, under the ancient oak. Mr. Chavez' watch said 3:29. Ortega would be sleeping in the kitchen. Ahmed would be in the storeroom, dreaming of desert nights. Rhino was the only member of the crew who made enough to keep his own place, which was a blue double-wide east of town.

176

PiGGS

All the girls were gone from Piggs. Cecil, Grape and Cat would be where they always were after closing time. They'd sit at Cecil's table, drinking and playing cards half the night. Grape wouldn't drink much, and Cat would curl up like a giant hound on the floor.

Jack peered in, to make certain they were all in place, then backed outside again. The night was extra dark, and the air was steamy hot. Jack's gut was knotted up tight, but he couldn't help that.

He stood against the corrugated wall for some time, breathing in and breathing out, staying in shadow, listening in the dark. A train rumbled by a mile off on the crossing, the road to I-35. Far down the street, a single traffic light blinked on and off.

Stand here forever, asshole, and you can blow it all off, say the time isn't right, you just need to wait it out...

He heard the sound then and froze. A shoe, scraping on the ground. And close, shit, right in the parking lot, only no one was there, everyone was gone!

Jack pressed himself against the wall. Looked to the right without moving his head. A car. Black Lincoln. Out on the edge of the lot, far from the 20-watt bulb that lit the front door at night.

Three guys. Four. One in the car, the others outside. One dragged on a smoke, lighting up his face.

Jack's heart nearly stopped. He knew who they were, who they had to be. It was Ambrose Junior's people— couldn't be anyone else just waiting out there.

Fuck, the deal was going down, it was going down tonight! If Cecil hadn't emptied his stash, he'd sure as hell do it now.

Jack clenched his fists until they hurt. It was hopeless, no way he could ever chance it now. Even if the stash was still there—which it wouldn't be, for sure—Cecil would catch him red-handed, would kill him without a blink.

177

It was over, then, done. Like all the other great plans since he'd been a hardass kid in Shawnee, Oklahoma. Something always went haywire, something always went wrong. And that something, a lot of the time, was him. Not always, maybe, sometimes another bozo helped, or a bottle or a woman came along, but he'd always sure as hell volunteered without ever looking back.

At least this was one time he knew when to quit, when the odds were too heavy even for a dumbshit like him. If Jesus wanted him to have a lot of dough and a girl like Gloria Mundi, he'd have worked something out before now. Before Jack went off to Huntsville prison. Before he started washing dishes at Wan's, taking shit off of Cecil R. Dupree. Riding fucking underage singers on his back.

Right?

Right.

So fuck it. Go for it. Death is just passing through one door and tripping through another. Ortega was always saying that, saying it didn't hurt at all. But what did Ortega know? The guy was a taco and didn't even speak his native tongue. Why would you listen to a dummy like that...?

THIRTY-ONE...

He had a strip of tin, bent and folded the way G.G. Perk had showed him to do. G.G. was doing twenty to life, and could open any door in the world except the ones he lived behind now.

Jack worked in the dark, hunched at the top of the stairs. He didn't use the flash. The stairs were just past the bar, and past that was Cecil, Grape and Cat. He could even hear them talk, which didn't help at all.

Sweat stung his eyes as he tried his pick in the first lock on the door. He couldn't read Mr. Chavez' expensive watch in the dark. What good was a watch, you couldn't see it in the dark? Fucking Mickey, you could see those little gloves in the dark, and it didn't cost a couple grand.

Ricky's gun was something else. It pressed against his ribs, and poked him in the groin. Rich guys had to have everything big. Big cars, big watches, big guns. You never see a rich guy driving a Geo, he's never got a little gun you can drop in your pocket somewhere.

The pick wouldn't go in the first lock, wouldn't even get past the front. Got it in the second but it wouldn't do shit. Rattled around and made a lot of noise.

He decided not to bother with the third. Two don't work, maybe one does. So what? So try it, you're here, okay?

The third one did the trick. Went in smooth as silk, *clack-clack-click,* like the pick and the lock were old friends.

Jack waited, listened for the voices down below, then gently turned the pick. The pick went *snap!* and broke off neatly in his hand.

Jack's gut began to churn, began to burn, began to go into its act. Jack held his breath, bit down the pain. He had to get down, without making a sound, tripping on something, maybe passing out.

Death, where the fuck you going to sting? That's another thing Ortega said that didn't make a bit of sense.

Then he did what everyone does, the thing you got to do when you know you been licked, when you can't get in the house, when you can't get in the car. You try the fucking knob, as a gesture of defiance, as a hopeless prayer that God will intercede this time, wake up a minute, and work his magic on the door. You know it's not about to happen, but it's human nature to try.

It opened without a sound...

The oldest gimmick in the book if you go to the movies, if you watch the TV, but art sticks a broken mirror up to life, as Ortega didn't say, but someone maybe did.

The next part was easy. Jack used his flash and went right to the spot where the trick board had to be. He stuck a fingernail in the crack and the panel slid away...

The box was still there.

Jack took a deep breath. If the box was still there, and the buy was going down, Cecil would be up those stairs any minute now. The box would be gone. Cecil R. Dupree would go bananas. He'd kill everyone in sight. Especially Jack, if he caught him up there.

He had to get out, get out of there fast. Get Mr. Chavez, get Ortega's car, drive the car to *Ricky's* car, get the hell out of Mexican Wells.

Jack pulled the box out of the hole. It was heavy, like it ought to be, a box full of that much dough. He set the box aside, replaced the panel in the floor. Didn't hear a thing until someone rattled the knob, someone opened the door.

Jack rolled, the box tucked into his belly, rolled behind the sofa as Cecil flipped the lights.

Jack froze, his hand on the grip of the heavy, silver-engraved weapon. The hammer caught in his belt, the sight stuck in his shorts. Cecil stomped about the room. Jack watched his shadow on the wall. Reached into his pants, freed the revolver and eased the weapon out.

Cecil walked to the far side of the room. Opened a closet, got something out, turned and started back. Jack, flat on his back, could see Cecil's big bare feet, the frayed cuffs of his overalls dragging on the floor.

Jack's gut went berserk. He knew what Cecil was doing, he was coming for the stash, coming for the money to make the buy.

Jack's hand tightened on the weapon. It would happen, happen in a minute, in a minute and a half. Cecil opens the panel, sees the box is gone. Yells and goes nuts, shouts for Grape and Cat. Jack shoots Cecil, so he won't have to take on all three.

Wait—they'll hear the shot, know he's in there. Jack has to chance it, whack them all at once. He's not Bruce Willis so he'll miss at least one—maybe all three. *Pow!* End of the movie, no more problems after that...

Jack gripped the Magnum, watched Cecil's feet. Cecil stopped. Waited a second, then turned and flipped the light and walked out the door.

Jack nearly lost it. Nearly threw up on Cecil's floor. Cecil didn't even *go* to the stash, he didn't get the money at all!

And Jack, several hundred rungs below Cecil on the ladder of crime, still knew at once what Cecil had in mind. That's what he was doing, stopping and thinking, in the middle of the room. He was thinking how he'd stiff the sellers, get the merchandise and keep the dough.

Cecil Dupree would do that. Cecil R. Dupree was crazy enough to try it, and crazy enough to bring it off...

❖ ❖ ❖

Jack used every ragged nerve he had left to get back down the stairs, and out the side door. Cecil, Grape and Cat were gone. Drinks left on the table. Peanuts, candy wrappers on the floor.

They were outside, then, meeting the Ambrose bunch. Jack kept close to the building, didn't even look at the lot, didn't take the shortcut to Wan's, went the long way around.

For a minute, he thought about Mr. Chavez, leaving him behind. What if someone saw him? The dumpster was close to the lot. The trouble was, the Mescan was the only person who could get him that offshore truss account, put his money safe somewhere so he and Gloria could get off to a good start. Without Ricky's help—

Jack's heart nearly stopped. Chavez was gone! Ragged strips of duct tape clinged to the dumpster, but the son of a bitch beaner was gone!

Jack backed away fast, turned and ran past Wan's, past the back lot and through the high weeds, juggling

Cecil's stash, tripping over bricks, bottles, tomato crates, all the crap Jack was supposed to haul away.

Fuck Chavez, Jack thought, he was on his own now. He couldn't have much of a start, and he wouldn't make it to his Park Avenue. It was too far to walk, even if you weren't stark naked——and besides, Jack had the keys. He could get to the Buick in Ortega's wreck in ten, fifteen minutes flat.

He paused, in the shadow of the live oak trees. Listened, couldn't hear a thing from Piggs. Good. That's what he wanted to hear. Nothing from Piggs, Wan's, Cecil, the whole bunch, ever again...

Ortega's car was gone.

Jack felt strangely calm. He wasn't angry, his stomach felt fine. He wasn't even greatly surprised. What the hell did he expect? Why should anything go right? You got a perfect run of bad luck, why break it now?

Okay, he had the gun, he had the stash. He could make it to the Park Avenue before it got light. Even if Chavez *tried* to get there, tried to get a ride—who'd pick up a naked Mescan in the middle of the night?

"No one in their fucking right mind," Jack thought, the words coming to him as the first harsh volley of shots echoed through the trees...

THIRTY-TWO...

W hat we going to do, we going to do it like they do on TV," said Hamilton T. Gerrard. "I'm the black dude, you the white guy. I put *my* stuff on the hood, you putting yours there too. Y'all with me so far?"

"Just do it," Cecil said. "I don't got to hear no rappity-rap, I don't got to hear no fucking soul."

Gerrard shook his head and grinned. "You are a difficult man to get along with, Mr. Dupree."

"Yeah, right. Let's see what you got, I'm tired of standing out here."

"Might think about *shoes,* Mr. Dupree. Meaning no offense."

Cecil didn't answer, and didn't take offense. He knew the routine, that's what you had to do. You do the talk, you knock the other guy, the other guy knocks you. The talk don't mean a thing. The talk lets you size the thing up. Same for the other guy, he's thinking too. Is he going to play it straight, or maybe try and take me down? Which one am *I* going to do?

So he talks to the nigger, the nigger talks to him. All the time they're talking, Cecil's taking in who the guy brought. The nigger's smart, Cecil's got to give him that. The bozos he's got are three white guys, and Cecil sees they've been there all along. The big guy was a trucker, one of the horsies from the race the night before. The other two were with him in the club tonight.

Cecil has thought about something like this. How anyone can come in the club, you don't know who they are. These three assholes are shooters, you can see that now, but if a guy's good, you got a hundred other guys drinking and yelling, it's fucking hard to tell.

The way it is, Cecil's leaning against his green Caddie, like he's maybe considering a nap. Cat's to his right, Grape's to his left. Just across from Cecil, Hamilton T. Gerrard is leaning on *his* car, looking cool and black. One of the truckers is standing on the far side of the Lincoln, watching Grape. The other two are just behind Gerrard. Everybody's got a gun, everybody knows that.

Cecil doesn't care it's four to three. It isn't how many, it's what's you do with what you got. Five to three, maybe, he wouldn't go for that.

"It's hot up here, isn't even light yet," said Hamilton Gerrard. "Don't see how you'all put up with it, Mr. Dupree."

"You got what, a fucking glacier in New Orleans, it's snowing down there?"

Gerrard smiled. One of the truckers started to laugh, but caught himself quick.

"We don't get out *in* it, Mr. Dupree. We stay in the AC. White tourist folks, they out in the heat. Willie Bee," Gerrard said, without taking his eyes off Cecil Dupree, "would you kindly get the merchandise out of the trunk, so me and my new friend can do some business here?"

Cecil flinched at the "friend" bit, but stood up straight, watching the bozo walk to the Lincoln's trunk. Grape moved a hair to the left. Even Cat had the sense to pay attention now.

The Lincoln was side-on to Cecil and his crew, but anything could happen, a guy's reaching in a trunk. He can come up with a missile, anything at all.

The guy was a pro. He took it slow and easy, brought out the attaché case in plain sight, laid it on the Lincoln's hood.

Hamilton T. Gerrard let his gaze flick from Cecil to Grape, Grape to the Cat, back to Cecil again. Everybody looked at everybody else, looked at everyone again.

"So, okay," Cecil said finally, "let's have a look. Maybe I'm buying today."

Gerrard raised a brow. "Let's look at *yours, Mr. Dupree.*"

Cecil didn't answer. He raised a brow back. Took a step away, turned and moved to the green Cadillac. Picked up an attaché sitting on the ground by the bumper, plainly in sight.

Hamilton T. Gerrard had seen him put it there, when Cecil and his crew came out of Piggs. He'd put it there till it was time to bring it out.

And Hamilton thought, as Cecil came toward him now, how *he* would have put the case just out of sight. Thought, too, he would've sent somebody, wouldn't go and pick it up himself.

... all this in a second, in a blur, little bright lights flick-flick in his head, then another after that, and this one fills him with awful dread...Cecil's smiling, happy as a clam, but that fucking mask isn't purple, isn't red anymore, it's as black as Gerrard's own skin...

Everything is flick-flick now, everything happens, turns to shit in a blink and a half.

◆ ◆ ◆

Grape knows how it goes down: When the deal's all over, things are cooling down, Grape pulls the Glock from his belt, takes out the guy on the left. Cat, who is broad enough to hide a tank, has a 12-gauge sawed-off hanging down his back. He takes out the bozos on the right. Cecil's got a blade, he does Hamilton T. Gerrard. This is how the thing's *supposed* to be, this is what they talked about, sitting there in Piggs…

…Three feet, two feet from Gerrard, Cecil lifts the case like it's going on the hood, next to the other case, where it ought to be. The .38 Charter is taped to the case, the side that Gerrard can't see. Gerrard can't see the gun, but he can see that face, and *knows* what Cecil's got in mind, knows this redneck fuck intends to kill him dead, just doesn't know how.

The .38 explodes, three blinding flares of white. Three frames of a mobster movie sear the night. Three very mean Hydra-Shoks, jacketed hollow-point, head for the gut of Hamilton Gerrard. When they hit, when they strike, they'll mushroom and make a horrid mess.

Hamilton's gone. Hamilton isn't there. He ducks to the right, turns his face aside, feels the heat of the little copper bees go by. One of the bees digs a furrow in the Lincoln's shiny hood. Two tear into the attaché and out the other side. The attaché erupts in a massive burst of coke, in a choking cloud of dope, in a cloud that would turn on Houston and half of San Antone.

Grape stumbles back. Can't believe his eyes. Sees Cat grab the sawed-off, jerks out the Glock, shoots Cat in the head. Cat staggers, takes a drunken step, goes over like an 18-wheeler truck.

Grape begins to shake, pees down his pants. "Aw, man," he groans, "what the fuck is *this…!*"

33

THIRTY-THREE...

Cecil is stunned, dizzy, totally out of synch. He can't see shit, he's white from head to toe. Hamilton Gerrard is white, too, but his face is still black, for he saw death coming and turned away in time.

Gerrard is no longer laid back, he is no longer cool, he is surely not happy, he is surely not fine. This is the *other* Hamilton T. Gerrard, the one who's foaming at the mouth, the one who's pleasant features are twisted in a dark, demonic rage.

The one who is kicking Cecil in the head, in the gut, in the crotch, anywhere he can.

Gerrard's three shooters blast away, firing into the pale narcotic cloud. Bullets whine this way and that. Into the cars, into the trees, into deepest inner space. One hits a bird in flight, one takes the "P" out of Piggs.

"Hold it, you fucking morons!" shouts Hamilton T. Gerrard. "You going to hurt somebody like that!"

The guns go silent. Cecil moans on the ground. Gerrard kicks him in the belly, kicks him soundly on the nose.

Squats down, opens Cecil's attaché case, stands up, brushes off his pants.

"Considering the circumstance, I am not surprised there isn't any money in here, isn't anything at all. Why you figure that is, Mr. Grape?"

Grape was more than uneasy, he was wet, shaken, purely terrified, certain he was close to being dead.

"Honest to God, Mr. Gerrard, I seen him go up, I seen him bring the case down..."

"You see anything *in* the case, Mr. Grape? You see about seventy-five grand?"

"No, sir. Mr. Cecil, he didn't show it to me."

"Carried it himself. Didn't show it to you."

"No, sir, he did not. Didn't show me nothing at all."

Grape looked at Cecil. Cecil looked bad. Didn't look at Cat.

"It wasn't supposed to go like that. We was supposed to take you out *after* the buy was done. I told Mr. Ambrose Junior on the phone. I didn't know nothing about this shit."

"Uh-huh."

"I had to take out Cat, Mr. Gerrard. You saw me do that!"

"I saw it." Hamilton T. Gerrard looked straight at Grape. "You betray Mr. Dupree, maybe you do the same to me."

"Hey, I'd be nuts to do that. I made a deal, you got to know I wouldn't do that."

"Don't know any such thing. Know my dope is blowing every which way. Know I got no money to show. I *know* Mr. Ambrose Junior going to ask me what kind of shit going on up here."

"Mr. Gerrard—"

"Bobby Cee, my man, Mr. Grape and I going to have a little talk inside. Keep an eye on Mr. Dupree here. Don't do him no hurt or anything. Mr. Ambrose Junior going to

see Mr. Dupree personal, seeing as how I don't intend to
take the flack for this fuckup myself. Mr. Grape, you kindly
come with me. See if we can maybe—*what the fuck! Mack,
Willie B.!*"

Gerrard stared, as headlights swung off the road and
seared his eyes. Gerrard's shooters scattered. One to the
left, one to the right. One stuck his pistol in the window of
a blue Toyota, yelled at the driver, told him to get the fuck
out.

The driver stepped out slowly, hands in the air. Looked
about, took in the scene, had an idea what was happening
here.

"Get your ass over here," Gerrard said. "Who you supposed to be?"

"Rhino," Rhino said. "I work here. Who the hell are
you?"

"He runs the Chink place, Mr. Gerrard," said Willie B.
"Food tastes like shit."

Gerrard looked Rhino up and down. "You work for Mr.
Dupree?"

Rhino looked at Cecil. "I don't guess I do."

"Your food as bad as Willie says?"

"Cook's an Ay-rab. What you going to do?"

Gerrard nodded. He seemed to understand. "You best
get inside with this other former em-ployee, it's getting
hot out here. We need to have a little—shit, Willie, where'd
Mr. Grape go? Find that little fuck, get him back here."

Gerrard shook his head. "This night has been an irritation to me. Don't guess it's going to get any better for a
while."

"You're from New Orleans, I guess," Rhino said. "I been
there. Isn't any hotter here."

"Don't start, Mr. Rhino. I am getting considerable tired
of hearing that..."

THIRTY-FOUR... 34

Jack could see the sky turning a liverish shade of purple, just above the top of Piggs. Only the sign read iggs, since those assholes had shot out the "P."

Lord God, if it wasn't a mess down there. He couldn't see it all from the trees, but he could see a lot more than he cared to see. Everyone started shooting, dope went everywhere. Cecil was on the ground, he couldn't see Cat anywhere. A skinny black dude was screaming at everyone, kicking at the ground...

"Fuck it," Jack said aloud, "I don't need this." He squinted at the dawn, turned and walked quickly back through the trees, picking up his steps, anxious to leave the whole business behind.

It wasn't hard to figure what to do next. Go. Just go. Head away from Piggs, keep out of sight. If he made it to Mr. Chavez' car, fine. Maybe he'd try and catch a ride. Stick up the driver. Make him go to Dallas, hole up there awhile. Maybe it'd be a good-looking babe. Maybe they'd talk, get along fine.

One thing he'd do as soon as he could was stop some-where, get a big screwdriver, some kind of pry. A tire tool'd do just fine. Carrying the box around was driving him nuts. It was like you *know* what you're getting, but you got to wait for Christmas to see. If he could just look at it, get a few bills in his pocket, put the rest back...

Jack stopped. Someone was up there, just past the trees. He listened, heard it again, something moving, something stirring up the dead leaves.

Drawing the big silver revolver from his belt, Jack carefully pulled a branch aside, took a cautious step, then another after that.

A twig snapped under his foot. Jack sprang back. Ricky Chavez whirled around and faced him, knees bent, gripping a piece of lumber, hard against his shoulder, like a naked Yankee, possibly a Met.

"*Dios,* Jack, what are you doing here!"

"I was going to ask you," Jack said. "Put that thing down, Mr. Chavez, I'm armed, as you can tell."

"You put down the revolver, Jack. Or give it to me, and I will happily kill you on the spot."

Jack lowered his weapon, but kept it at his side.

"I'd like to know how you got loose. That duct tape was on there tight."

"There are many rusty cans by the place of the dumpster."

"I didn't think of that. I was—aw, man, who's that? What'd you do, Mr. Chavez?"

Jack's stomach did a flip. He knew who it was, didn't have to ask. Grape was sprawled in the brush. His eyes were open and he looked real surprised. His neck was turned in an odd direction, one Jack knew wasn't right.

"He came upon me. I was resting at the moment, he is coming through the woods."

"You hit him with that."

Ricky looked disturbed. "He said he had never seen a naked greaser before. One with very small—private parts."

"You look okay to me. Not that I'd care if you do or not."

"It is most improper to speak of a man's *pene,* Jack. I was quite humiliated. I do not think I would have reacted so strongly if I had not had such a bad day."

"I feel partially responsible for that."

"I feel this is true. You have the money there?"

"I got it, all right. I didn't screw up that."

"How much is there?"

"I don't know. I got to get something to pry off the lock. I got your car keys, Mr. Chavez. But it's a hell of a walk."

"I cannot go anywhere like this. I must have clothes of some sort."

"A lot of the time, your fugitives on TV will steal clothes off a line. We might run across a farm somewhere."

"I think people do not use the lines anymore. I think they use the *máquina de lavar,* the laundromat."

"Yeah, okay, we can do that."

Ricky turned the thick club in his hands. Started to drop it, decided to keep it a while.

"There was a great disturbance at Piggs. What exactly occurred back there?"

"We'll get you some clothes, I'll tell you about it. You going to hold onto that?"

"Yes. I feel that I am."

"You first, then. I'll keep an eye out behind..."

◆ ◆ ◆

Ortega guessed it was nine. He didn't have a watch, and the clock in the Plymouth hadn't worked since 1989, when he bought the car secondhand. He guessed it was nine, because the heat wasn't rising off the road, and the tar didn't really start to melt until ten.

Another sign was he wished he was dead. Drink all night and watch the sun rise, you know there's no point in being alive. Worse still, he'd let Ahmed come along. He didn't like Ahmed, and Ahmed didn't like him. But Ahmed had money at the time, and Ortega had a car, and life is full of compromise.

Ortega swore this was something he'd never do again. After two beers, Ahmed started singing, songs from Iraq with a military bent. The bar was called Tejas Tel Aviv, and some of the patrons had strong opinions about the Middle East.

Ortega slowed before he got to his place beneath the ancient oak tree. Slowed, because he didn't like the look of things at Piggs.

"I don't like the look of things," he said. "Doesn't look right to me."

"W'at it lookin' like to you? Ees lookin' like Piggs to me."

"That's because you don't look. There's nobody *here.* Nobody here, nobody at Wan's. There's nothing in the lot but Cecil's car."

"Is a tit bar an' a res'rant, man. Ees nothin' to do when the sun coming up."

"There's always someone, though. Grape's van, the guy brings the beer, someone hanging around."

Ortega pulled up behind Cecil's alligator-green Cadillac, got out and closed the door. Ahmed groaned, got out the other side, peed on the asphalt, squinted at the sun. In the desert, it would be about a hundred and ten. In Mexican Wells it was nice in the morning, maybe ninety-two.

"You can mess 'round all you want. I t'ink I go an' wake up Jhack. I am not sleeping, Jhack, he is goin' to be awake too—"

"Shit, oh shit, Ahmed, come look at this!"

"Looka what?" Ahmed zipped up, muttered to himself. Ortega had opened the back door of Cecil's car.

"Oh, sheet," Ahmed said, "looka dat."

"That's what I said. Don't say what I said, say somethin' else."

Ahmed could scarcely recall when he didn't have something to say. Now was maybe, four, maybe six times. Cat sat in the car, staring straight ahead, all the color drained from his face. His enormous bulk took up the back seat. He always smelled very bad, but he smelled really awful today.

"Hi, Ahmed. Hi, Ortega. It's me," Cat said.

Ortega almost jumped at the voice. It sounded like a frog had crawled inside his head.

"You don't sound good. You don't look good, too. I think you got a hole in your head."

"Tha's w'at he got, he got thees hole in the haid."

"What happened," Ortega said, "what the hell happened here, where's everybody at?"

Ortega leaned in closer, suddenly wary, suddenly certain he was right to have a bad feeling about this very hot morning at Piggs.

The hole in Cat's head was ugly and dark. A crater, a pit, dry and crusty on the rim, shading down to black. In the center, Ortega could see something shiny, something bright, something the color of lead.

"What I think," he told Ahmed, "I think that Cat has been shot. I think he's been shot in the head."

"I am agree wit' dis," Ahmed said.

"What happened Cat, can you say? Who did this to you?"

"Hosa...hosa-piddle."

"What?"

"Hosa...hosa..."

"Hospital, yes? You want to go to the hospital. This is what you're saying."

"You crazy or w'at? I am helpin' de Cat? Give me a ghon, I shoot heem agin."

"He's a real asshole, all right. But he's a human being like us. We'll have to take him in this car. Couldn't both of us move him into mine."

Ahmed looked stricken. "We are drivin' Cecil's car? Now I know you 'pletely nuts."

Ortega was already around the side, in the driver's seat. He found the key on the mat. Started the Caddie up. Groaned, and slapped the wheel.

"Damn thing is nearly empty. We are not driving very far."

"Good. We try an' do the erran' of mercy, we have fail. That settle dat."

"You got money, we can get some gas."

"I got twenny, t'irty cents. You drink eet all up."

"Least I can finish more than two beers."

"Thass a beeg lie. I drink six, maybe ten."

"You didn't even get to three—"

"Muuuny..."

"What?" Ortega leaned over the back to look at Cat. "What you saying? What you trying to say, man?"

"M-m-misster Cecil...he gonna len' Cat a dollah...won' mind..."

"Yeah, right. Well Mr. Fucking Cecil isn't here right now, and I am not about to go and look."

"Focking right, mahn."

"Won' mind...len' it tah me..."

"Look, man..."

Cat's eyes crossed twice. His face filled with agony, twisted with pain. He lifted a great paw, lifted it with torturous effort, reached out and dug his fingers into the panel of the door. Struggled, groaned, sweat popped out on his brow.

Plastic ripped and tore. The door handle snapped, dropped and fell away. With a final, wrenching sound, the panel burst free.

Money dropped in Cat's lap, rushed, tumbled, spilled in a green avalanche to the floor, rolled out on the ground. Twenties, hundreds, an endless flow, pack after pack of lovely bills.

"Holy shit," Ortega said.

"Holy sheet," Ahmed said too.

"Munny..." Cat said.

"That son of a bitch," Ortega said. "That sly old bastard hid his dough in the fucking car. The dummy saw him, and put it there."

Ortega picked up a stack of fifties, tried to do something in his head. Gave up, looked at Ahmed.

"I think I will go home again. It has been a long time."

"I never have be to Mexico."

"Wisconsin. I got roots, I got family there."

"I am t'inking Califor'ya. I am t'inking the beech, I am t'inking the gorls."

"Hosa-piddle," Cat said.

"Focking right. Hosa-piddle, mahn..."

OPENING NIGHT...

Iggs didn't make a lot of sense, and Rhino thought about Niggs, or Jiggs, but only to himself, not to anybody else, and certainly not to Mr. Hamilton T. Gerrard. They'd never talked about it, but Rhino had an idea racial humor wasn't a topic his boss would care about at all.

What he did was take the neon "W" from Wan's, and call the place Wiggs. No one asked what it meant, no one seemed to care. That left an's for the restaurant, which wasn't Chink anymore, but kind of Creole-Thai, and seemed to fit.

The little blue pigs stilled blinked and whirled around Wiggs, but that was fine, too. Guys came to drink and see bare-ass girls. The philosophy of signs was the farthest thing from their minds.

Mr. Gerrard said Mr. Junior Ambrose didn't much like baby pigs. What Mr. Ambrose liked were gators, and Mr. Gerrard brought a pickup full from Louisiana, where gators were easy to find. They looked real nice behind glass, and Mr. Gerrard had a decorator person from Dallas come in, and install some plastic plants.

Very few patrons asked to sign a gator. When anyone did, Rhino had them shown to the door. Mostly, he roamed around in a new sportcoat and a tie for every night. He greeted everybody, watched the money flow, kept a close eye on the bar.

The everyday work he left to his assistant manager. Jack did a real good job, keeping up the inventory, making sure the waiters and the cooks didn't kill each other, or steal more than they should.

Jack got along well with the girls, and Rhino was happy to leave the job to him. Women were fine, but fussing with them was an irritation Rhino could do without.

He walked around Wiggs, looked at the tables, looked at the bar. Checked the restrooms to make sure no one was about. Seeing the place empty didn't seem right, but it was just for the night, and he guessed he could put up with that.

Peering across the way, he saw Jack had closed up an's, locked it up tight. It was good to have someone you could trust, leave things to, know they would all go right.

Rhino knew people. He'd always had this rare insight. Right from the start, he knew Jack had what it took. No one else saw it, but Rhino did. What it was was a gift. You either had it or not, you couldn't learn something like that...

◆ ◆ ◆

That magic moment just before dark was Jack's favorite time of day. It seemed like the world kind of paused and held its breath, before the light slid away. It had finally rained in Mexican Wells, and everything was green and bright.

He had always thought there was no better way to see the countryside than from a car. Walking, you got tired of seeing one thing. Driving, stuff changed all the time. He was grateful to Rhino, who'd let him have his '95 Toyota on time, when he'd bought his new Cad. He could handle the payments on his salary, and what he siphoned off on the side. A little from the till, and kickbacks from the meat and beer guys.

Mostly, he thought, things were going fine. He'd never imagined he could live without Gloria Mundi, but that was working out okay. The new girl from Wichita Falls, JoAnn Sebastian Box, was a honey and a half, and it looked like she cared for him too.

Sometimes he thought about Cecil's stash, and regretted it had turned out that way. But the past was gone and you had to look back, as Ortega used to say. Mr. Chavez told Jack he'd made a real find. Cecil's baseball cards dated back to the 1900s, and some of them were signed. Mr. Chavez gave him three hundred dollars for the lot—which told Jack what he already knew, that Mescans weren't nearly as smart as they thought.

"What I want you to do," Jack said, "I want you first thing in the morning, I want you to get that shit out of the storeroom, out back where it belongs. Then you get the kitchen stocked, and I want it fucking neat. N.E.A.T. neat. Don't you fucking forget."

"Uhhhhnnn...uhhhnnnn..."

"You say *yes,* damn it, don't give me that uhhhnnn-uhhhnn business. You say it. You say 'yes.'"

"Yuuuuuush..."

"Okay, that's a start. You are an aggravation to me, I don't mind saying that."

Cecil sat in back, all hunched over, all crouched up, flapping his arms like a fucking chicken, twitching and blinking like he always did. Son of a bitch couldn't look at you straight. His eyes were all gotchy, like where a rock hits the windshield when you're going too fast. He sure wasn't the Cecil he'd been before they took him to New Orleans, but no one complained about that.

Jack didn't miss the old Cecil, he sure as hell didn't miss Grape. Whatever they'd done with Cat, Jack didn't care, and didn't ask. He hated to say it, but sometimes he missed Ortega and Ahmed, and wondered where they'd gone. The new guys were better, but one was a pure albino, and the other was a Jap.

"Uhhhhhnnnn...uhhhnnnnn..." Cecil said, and Jack said, "I see it, shut the fuck up back there."

Jack had to admit the place really looked fine. **THE BATTLE OF BRITUN FAMILY FUN PARK** sparkled like a Christmas tree, all shiny and bright. Cars were parked everywhere, as people flocked from all over to see the wonders of Opening Night.

Even from the parking lot, Jack could see the "Loopin' Stuka" ride, streaking by on tracks above the park. Closer, he caught the "Howlin' Hawker Hurricanes" whirling screaming kids about. The night was alive with the sound of dogfights shrieking through speakers set up in the trees.

Ricky Chavez had done a great job, you had to give him that. It took a lot of money, but the place looked grand.

Jack didn't need a ticket. He knew nearly everyone who worked on the grounds. Most of the staff were high school and college kids from Mexican Wells, Luling, San Marcos, and San Antone. The boys were all pilots, and the girls were nurses of many nations, Allied and Axis Powers alike.

Cecil went "Uhhhhnnnn...uhhhhnnn," and tried to hop away to a hot dog stand.

"Damn it, we'll get something later, you stick with me now."

There were plenty of things to eat, and a hundred different smells wafted through the air. Everything from American burgers to Nazi schnitzel, and RAF kidney pie.

Jack couldn't help it. When he spotted Gloria through the crowd, his heart skipped a beat. Lord, she looked fine. She had on a 1942 dress with the big shoulder pads, and a funny little hat. She wasn't that far along yet, and the baby didn't show.

Ricky looked handsome and gallant in his natty Luftwaffe blues. Gloria gazed up at him with an almost mystical sparkle in her eyes, and Jack couldn't deny they belonged together now. She wasn't his, and they'd never go for pie, but he'd always remember those special moments when she looked in the mirror, and her robe slid to the floor.

"Uhhhhnnn...uhhhnnn...uhhnnnn!" said Cecil, and tugged at Jack's sleeve.

"Stop it," Jack said, slapping Cecil's hand aside. "I 'bout had enough of you." He looked down at Cecil, and Cecil looked up at him.

"Get down," Jack said. Get down now. You know what to do."

"Uhhhhnnn...uhhhnn..." Cecil showed Jack a glassy stare, and flapped his arms in alarm.

"Do it, Cecil, don't you mess with me."

Cecil mumbled and whined, but did as he was told. And when he was down on all fours, Jack drew a short iron rod from his belt, a piece he'd found behind an's, and carried all the time.

Then, as Messerschmitts and Spitfires snarled overhead, as children and grown-ups crowded in to watch, Jack mounted up, kicked Cecil in the sides, and gave him a healthy whack.

"Hi ho," he shouted to the night, "Hi ho, motherfucker, hu-wayyy...!"